# DEATH CALLING

She noticed the light on her answering machine flashing silently. She grabbed her pad and a pencil and sat on the top of the table. Then she reached over to punch the silver bar.

The voice was raspy and hoarse. Disguised somehow. The pen fell from her hand and rolled unnoticed across the floor.

"I'm calling to tell you I'm going to kill you. Your days are numbered. When you least expect it, you're going to die. Pray for yourself, B.J. No one else can."

The message ended, the machine beeped, and B.J. screamed out loud, stuffing her fist into her mouth. Then calm silence returned to the house.

# Cry in the Night

## JUDI MILLER

AVON BOOKS ◆ NEW YORK

AVON BOOKS
A division of
The Hearst Corporation
105 Madison Avenue
New York, New York 10016

Copyright © 1990 by Judi Miller
Front cover illustration by Tim O'Brien
Published by arrangement with the author
Library of Congress Catalog Card Number: 89-91868
ISBN: 0-380-75699-4

First Avon Books Printing: March 1990

AVON TRADEMARK REG. U.S. PAT. OFF. AND IN OTHER COUNTRIES, MARCA REGISTRADA, HECHO EN U.S.A.

Printed in the U.S.A.

RA 10 9 8 7 6 5 4 3 2 1

*For all of us who remember Madison*

# Prologue

## 1963

THE two coffins lay facing each other in the living room. It was September and the morning sunshine shone brightly, bathing the room with warmth. The beauty of the sun almost defied the grim reality. One coffin was open; the other was sealed shut.

Guests were starting to come in to pay their last respects. The men put their hats on the mantel. The ladies dressed in their churchgoing clothes kept their hats on.

Grandfather sat alone to the side. Maxwell Stronger fondled the cold metal of his one-prong walker. His arthritis had been acting up. Ever since the state trooper had appeared at their door two nights ago to ask if they could identify two bodies found in a car crash on Route 20.

"Can't do that, officer. You see, they were going on vacation, left the little ones with us for a short spell," Max had said stubbornly. "They're on the way to Atlantic City. Probably there by now. Look here, young feller, I'll call their hotel and you can talk to them yourself." He hobbled over to the living room as the state trooper turned his hat in his hands, familiar with the scene he was witnessing now. Stronger let the phone ring and after the hotel finally answered he had said,

"I see, thank you." He threw up his arms in defeat. "I guess they're just not there yet. With weather like this, can you blame them? Probably stopped for coffee or dinner. You come by tomorrow and I'll let you talk to them."

Maxwell Stronger never saw the bodies at the morgue in Painseville. He sent his wife. Mary was ten years younger.

He sat staring now at the shiny pine coffin. John had been in his prime, did real well at that fancy real estate office and he had investments he guarded closely. John was very clever with money but he wouldn't let on.

He hid his face in his hands. He hadn't been to church in ten years. He'd let Mary go for him. Maybe what had happened was the punishment from God for his sin, his and Mary's.

A woman with a black hat with a big feather tapped him on the shoulder. "It's a shame," she said. "We heard it on the radio. Right on 20. The state should fix that highway."

Mary Stronger, her hair prematurely white, making her look almost seventy, sat in the front room, staring at the coffins like her husband. She had wanted to have another look at her son but the coroner suggested the coffin be closed.

But she had dressed them both for company. John, or what was left of him, was wearing a navy suit and burgundy tie, though only the maggots would see him. All the guests could see was a closed coffin. The wife was dressed in her wedding gown with white ribbons in her light brown hair. On her feet she wore white-and-gold sandals. Kind of a waste of time, she had thought, but a wake was a wake.

Some of the mourners who had walked over, who lived right on Madison-on-the-Lake, whose children had gone to Madison High with the dead man, sat and cried. It could have been one of their children. Most of them were married. Many had left Madison, Ohio. That's why this had happened, she was sure of it. John had left home.

The living room was stuffed with people. The class of Madison '53 was there. Her people weren't there. John had married a woman whose parents had totally disowned her for marrying a boy so totally beneath her. As many could come came. There wasn't a dry eye in the place. Both John Stronger and his pretty wife were dead. But she was a Cleveland girl, Shaker Heights.

"So young," someone whispered out loud. Everyone turned.

Mary Stronger couldn't help but wish that it been just Betty Jo who had had her life snuffed out like that when she was only in her mid twenties. John was at his peak. Her only adored son. She had never liked her daughter-in-law and her snooty ways.

She sighed and someone reached out to pat her on the shoulder. She had to give that Betty Jo credit when all was said and done: She had gone for the deal they had all made together. Yes, she had agreed.

At that moment with the living room swelling with sweating mourners, the little girl ran into the room. It was hushed as she stopped at her mother's coffin and tried to wake her up. "Mama, mama?" she demanded, lifting her dress, and with fat little legs tried to get in. "Mama, mama?" she demanded, "wakeup, wakeup," as she wept piteously and so did most of the adults in the room.

More than one pair of hands reached to pull her back.

"Mama's quiet now, honey, come over here and sit by Clara."

The little girl ran in her flouncy pumpkin-colored dress to her grandmother, who didn't lift her arms, who just sat crying and confused. Someone quickly grabbed her up. "Look here, what a pretty little dress. Spittin' image of your mama."

3

Someone in the back wept for the heartbreak of it all.

The little girl broke free and ran up to the coffin again. She banged her little fists on the side of the box.

"Daddy!" the little girl screamed.

"Daddy's in the other nice box, sweetie pie. Daddy and Mama are going to heaven and if you're a good little girl, they'll come back and visit you in their dreams," a nice lady said.

A teenage girl rushed in holding a coloring book and a box of crayons.

"I'm paying you to watch her and then she comes down here and makes a ruckus. She's a bad little girl. I won't have spoiled children." Mary Stronger stood with her hands on her hips.

"Yes, ma'am," the teenager said. "Come and play with your brother like a good girl."

"I ain't upstairs," said a little boy of about eight. "I'm sittin' right here watching the show. Seems to me like my folks are dead as doornails. We going to live in Madison with the grandparents?"

"Upstairs, scoot," said the baby-sitter. The smell of death made her dizzy. She wished she hadn't accepted this job.

The doorbell rang and the funeral began. The smaller coffin was closed, the top biting a white and light blue ribbon. Strong arms lifted the coffins out of the living room and into the hearses. The cemetery was all the way to Union City.

It was still blazing sunshine when they arrived at the site of the family plot now bedecked with healthy greenery. The mourner made a small path for Maxwell and Mary Stronger, she leaning on him and he leaning on a four-pronged walker.

The big old house on the corner of Easton and Hall near the lake was shockingly quiet once everybody left. The baby-sitter picked up the little girl and took her up

4

to the attic to play. There were mountains to climb in the attic. Old lamps, a broken couch, a tall hat rack, pictures.

"Mama," said the little girl, pointing to a framed photograph that had been hastily stashed.

"Talk, dummy," said the gangling ten-year-old boy.

"C'mon, Wilton. She's lost her mama and daddy and she's only three."

"Mama," the little girl screeched. "I want my mama."

Wilton put his fingers in his ears. "Shut up!" he shouted. "A boy wouldn't do that. But you're only a girl."

When she left the little girl to pay some attention to Wilton, she gave her a coloring book and some Crayolas, hoping that would calm her down. Suddenly she looked over and saw that the tiny girl was ripping her coloring book so that there was a pile of shredded paper on the dirty wooden floor. She noticed the pretty little girl lift her little dress and pull down her cotton panties. Then she watched horrified as the little girl put a crayon in her vagina so it stuck out like a little penis. "Now Willie like me," she said proudly, and giggled.

He laughed and somehow the baby-sitter sensed that she had done this trick before. She looked over at the little boy, who was smiling.

"No, B.J., naughty girl. You must never stick anything up there. It's dirty."

The baby-sitter pulled out the sticky crayon and tossed it aside. Then she picked up the underpants and slid them back up. The little girl stood wide-eyed and sucked her thumb.

Even through the tiny attic window they could see it was starting to get dark. How many hours had they played in the attic? How long did it take to bury people, the baby-sitter wondered.

"I'm hungry," Wilton said loudly.

"Let's turn on the television," the baby-sitter said. "And I'll see what there is to eat."

"There's no television," Wilton said when she started to go downstairs. "Grandma and Grandpa like to listen to the radio like the good old days."

The baby-sitter nodded. She looked down at the miserable little girl who would not stop crying.

The baby-sitter looked dismally at her watch and then herded her two charges down the steep, slanty steps, to the kitchen with its antique stove and noisy refrigerator. Their larder was empty except for bologna and cheese and white bread. No juice, no milk. The baby-sitter shivered even though the May temperature was balmy. She also found a big box of Kellogg's corn flakes, which they ate like popcorn.

"Okay, you kids," the baby-sitter said with new-found authority. "Now I want youse guys to take a bath. Okay?"

"It's too early to go to bed."

"How do you know what time it is, smartie?" the baby-sitter asked. "Do you have a watch on?"

"I just know."

They all climbed back up the stairs to the second-floor bathroom, where there was a wide tub with big brass feet that looked like claws. The now harassed baby-sitter undressed both children quickly and put them in the tub together, bending over to scrub them both. The little girl was by now giggling as she tried to snatch the slippery soap.

At that moment the grandmother walked in.

Her face was flushed with outrage.

"Take those children out of the tub and cover their nakedness. Then come downstairs and I'll pay you your money and you can leave."

She marched out of the room as the baby-sitter protested, "But I was only giving them a bath. After all, they *are* brother and sister."

"You don't understand," the grandmother said at the top of the steps. "It can't be."

The woman was still angry and upset when the baby-sitter left knowing she had been shortchanged. Once or twice they called her back but she wouldn't go to that house. In all her years of Madison High, before she grew up and moved away, she could never remember having a stranger baby-sitting job.

# BOOK
# I

# Chapter One

## *May: 1978*

MADISON-ON-THE-LAKE, Ohio, started at the railroad tracks at the top of the hill and went right down to the shore of Lake Erie. The road along the lake was full of hidden bumps and if you timed it right it had the effect of a roller-coaster ride. As soon as the kids grew up they took cars and motorcycles and even bikes and raced over the tiny hills as fast as they could, laughing all the way.

The kids were a gang of children who had started to play together when they were very young. They, all of them, became the very best of summer friends. The kids were made up of Townies and Summers since Madison was a resort town. The Summers came from places like Shaker Heights and other suburbs of Cleveland and had winterized cottages with closed-in patios and a television in every bedroom. The Townies lived there all year round, knew how to walk barefoot fearlessly, ride a horse without a saddle, and find the best blackberry patches.

It was a month before graduation from high school. Some of the Summers were going to Europe before starting college. Some had summer jobs in Cleveland. The Townies vied for the jobs in Madison. The frozen custard stand, the Bluebird Inn, the library.

The kids were breaking up. After this summer they probably wouldn't see each other at all. It was sad in its way.

On a chilly day in May, Hugh, who was a Summer, and Frank, who was a Townie, practically bumped into each other on Lake Road in front of the frozen custard stand. The music on the loudspeaker was blaring out a Sinatra tune. "Hey, man," Frank said, grabbing the other boy's arm. "What are you doing out here so early? Lookin' for some pussy?"

Hugh looked at the boy, squinted, blushed, and then laughed loudly. "No, we came out to put the old place up for sale. I'm going to Harvard in September. Mother says the cottage was for the kids, anyway."

"Harvard," Frank said. "That's nice." His black hair had been cut short and he was wearing jeans cut off at the knee. His T-shirt was rolled up at the arms.

"Yeah, Harvard and then law school."

Frank shook his head. Then he started to laugh. "Say, do you remember the year when you were flunking math and your parents were afraid you'd have to stay home and go to summer school and that would have messed up the summer for everybody?"

Hugh sighed. "That was a long time ago. It was like eighth grade."

Frank was still laughing. "So we all got together on the beach the weekend before and coached you. And you passed. Barely. So how much did your parents have to bribe Harvard to let you in, huh?"

Both boys laughed but Hugh was hoping Frank would just leave. It had started last summer, his feeling about Frank. About feeling embarrassment around him.

"You going to Ohio State?" Hugh asked politely.

"Well, not this year Hughie. I'll probably work this year and go next year."

Hugh nodded. "That sounds great. Ohio State is a

really good school. Hey, have you seen any of the kids today?''

"Only B.J.'' Frank said and Hugh felt his heart do a nosedive. They were standing on the top of the steep cliff that separated the township park from the beach with its receding shoreline. "There she is. The only one on the beach.''

Hugh couldn't take his eyes off the shiny blue swimming suit she wore. Even from there she looked gorgeous. She was the most beautiful woman he had ever known. All that Madison-less winter he had lain there in bed, lights out, thinking of her, pajama bottoms rolled down, vaseline under the bed.

He was hoping to see her this weekend. Just to get closer. It was so hard to know B.J. First there was her bad homelife. But after all, he just wanted to touch her, press her against him, feel his lips on her skin. Just once before he left Madison probably for good. Of course he wouldn't hurt her. She would have fun, too.

She was on the beach. That was convenient. He didn't want to seem too obvious.

"Waiting for someone?'' Hugh asked Frank with a silly little smile on his face.

"Just taking a little walk to the general store. You?''

"Just passing by,'' Hugh said as B.J. came up.

"Well, if it isn't the Gruesome Twosome. What happened, Hughie? They kick you out of Shaker Heights High before graduation?''

Both boys smiled. B.J. grinned at them. She was wearing a towel around her middle and a one-piece bathing suit that strained to cover her breasts. Her sea-blue eyes resembled the beach glass they occasionally found along the shore. Her skin was a golden peaches-and-cream. Her black sooty eyelashes were just that way. She wore no makeup. Her blond hair was streaked by the sun from ash to flaxen. Hugh saw that she had changed again this winter and she was more gorgeous than ever, almost luminescent. He had to have her. And he was used to getting what he wanted.

"I'm out for the weekend. My parents are packing it in." He couldn't help but stare at her. This was the skinny kid they had all protected, trying to make up for her grim homelife. He could tell she didn't yet know the effect she had on men. That made her all the more desirable.

"I guess that's the end of us kids," B.J. said sadly.

Both boys were quiet. The top flap of her bathing suit lifted in the breeze and they tried hard not to stare at it, failing miserably.

"Do you have a mantra when you meditate?"

B.J. laughed at them. "No I just concentrate on the highest wave in the lake, like I was riding it."

The boys laughed with her. Hugh felt again he couldn't make conversation with her. She was even kookier than in other years. "I don't do it right but I love it. It relaxes me. I like it."

"Listen, Beej, I'm only in for tonight and tomorrow and I won't be out this summer. Why don't you let me buy you dinner for old times' sake?"

"I can't, Hughie. I have a baby-sitting job tonight."

"Well, where is it?" he asked.

Frank lit a cigarette, stealing glances at his summer pal.

"Oh, it's beyond the Rabbit Run Theatre. It's the old Nixon property, the house with lavender shutters." She thought a minute. "But I can't have company when I baby-sit," she said.

"No, of course not," Frank said.

"It wouldn't be right," Hugh agreed.

"I gotta go, kids. They'll start missing Cinderella."

"Where are you working this summer, Beej?" Frank asked.

B.J. shrugged. "I don't know yet."

She waved goodbye to the boys and walked away,

her towel tight over her rear and swaying with her body. One or two people turned to look as she walked by.

The two boys stared after her.

Then Frank clapped Hugh on the shoulder. "Have time for a beer over at the Bluebird?" They never asked for ID from the kids they knew.

"Nah, I have to help my mom with stuff."

Frank was quiet and then he said speedily, "Listen, you aren't, you know, interested in B.J. or anything, are you?"

Hugh laughed and was embarrassed that the pitch of his voice came out like a falsetto. "No," he said. "I have a girlfriend in Cleveland."

"Yeah, me neither," Frank said. "She's got enough problems without us, agreed?"

The boys shook hands but they followed B.J. with their eyes until all they could make out was a blue dot.

B.J. had already forgotten about them. She would miss the kids but she had never really truly felt a part of them. It was more that they had always included her. They felt sorry for her and she hated that.

As she came to the row of wooden bathhouses that had once been a sparkling white in the days of the ancient Madison Country Club, she put her towel around her shoulders. From the late thirties to the early fifties there had been croquet and badminton on the lawn, and sailboats on the lake when it looked as clear as a sheet of ice. Then one year there had been a murder in the row of clean white houses. It was just so incongruous. Those things never happened in Madison.

Nothing ever happened in Madison.

That was why she was leaving. The day after graduation she would flag down the Greyhound bus and go to Cleveland. From Cleveland she would take a bus to New York City. Ever since she had been five she had known what she wanted to be. She wanted to become an actress. She had saved her money from the baby-sitting jobs. Even though her grandmother had made her give over half, she still had enough to get to New York and find a room. She was going to get a job and study at the American Academy of Dramatics, where all those famous stars had gone.

Only, it was a secret.

No one knew. If anyone knew they would gossip, and if her grandparents found out they would try to stop her. She couldn't tell anyone.

In a way she liked that better.

*Actress.* She liked the sound of the word. She knew she was good. She had never been allowed to appear in the Madison High plays but she knew she could do it. She had taken play books from the library and read all the good parts out loud.

And then the miracle had happened last term. She had started to change. About fifteen pounds had miraculously dropped off but her bra size had increased. Her complexion seemed to clear up on its own and suddenly she noticed that men would say silly things just to get nearer to her.

A lot of the girls in Madison High didn't like her. She pretended not to care but she did, very much. Everyone would be sorry for snubbing her because one day she would be a big star.

Past the country club, past the general store, which sold everything from shoelaces to beer, past the gas station was her house: the shabby one-floor house that needed painting, with the untrimmed shrubbery. As usual, her stomach muscles tightened and again she thought what her life might have been like had her parents survived the automobile crash.

In the first year they had kept a framed wedding portrait on the mantel. Her mother had had her arm around her father and they were both laughing about something. But one day the picture had disappeared and she had never found it. Now she had forgotten what they had looked like.

They wanted to marry her off, her grandparents did. So every Wednesday night Edward Bailey came to dinner. They ate in the dining room. He was a man in his thirties with thinning hair who had said he would marry her after her graduation.

B.J. shut her eyes. The smell of Edward Bailey was the smell of death. He was an embalmer at the new funeral parlor in North Madison and she could smell the chemicals on him like an after-shave lotion. She couldn't stand the way he looked at her, as though she were a fat, juicy pig waiting to be slaughtered. She had no intention of marrying the man.

B.J. ran into her room and changed into jeans and a T-shirt. She could hear the television blaring loudly in the living room. It must have been around 1970 when her grandparents took the van into Painseville and picked up a black-and-white TV. Since then, their lives had changed. All day they watched it. They each had an armchair. If you tried to interrupt them you were confronted with a veil of silence.

B.J. went into the kitchen. Wilton was on the phone, speaking in a low voice, the receiver cradled to his ear. He pointed to the sink. B.J. saw the mound of dirty dishes piled high.

She sighed and picked up the sponge and a bottle of detergent. Wilton was grinning and holding the phone close to his ear.

"Oh, c'mon, baby, it wasn't that bad. Now, you know it didn't hurt. You loved it. Next time it will be better. Now we have to go to the drive-in. We still didn't see the movie." He laughed then whispered, "Do I love you?" His voice was brittle. "You know I do, baby."

B.J. scrubbed a pot, thinking how hard Wilton's laugh was. It was a mean laugh. There wasn't anything

17

joyful about it. She had been the brunt many times. When they were little he would belittle her in front of company and he would have that laugh; and humiliated, she would cry.

Wilton looked up and pointed to the floor. B.J. knew what he meant. She listened as he dialed another number. "Aw, baby, can't you get some of those birth control pills? I ain't gonna get you into trouble. I know how to do it." Again his voice was soft, urgent, private. It was as if B.J. wasn't there, couldn't even hear him. She felt like the maid.

She made a face at him. Then she looked up.

Grandmother was staring at her.

"Don't you make faces at your brother, miss. He works hard. If it wasn't for his job at the gas station, you wouldn't eat so good, lady."

She moved closer to the sink, her sour breath making B.J.'s nose crinkle. Then she grabbed hold of B.J.'s arm, underneath her T-shirt, until B.J. wanted to cry out.

"Listen, missy," she said, "Edward Bailey told me he wants to marry you. He'll pay off our mortgage if he can. What have you got better? Those fancy summer friends of yours aren't going to give you a tumble. You're not their type, girl. And as for those young bucks around Madison, those boys are good for nothing. And I don't want no bastard children around here." She spat out the last remark like an accusation.

B.J. winced as the old woman yanked her hair and pulled. "You listen to me. He's a good catch. You'll thank me one day, girl."

Her grandmother, who was in her seventies, let go of B.J.'s hair. B.J. exhaled the air she had sucked in and said what she had learned to say a long time ago: "Yes, ma'am."

Then she calmly turned back to the putrid-smelling dishes. She knew what she was going to do. The day

18

after graduation, she'd be on Route 20 heading for a brand-new future, and nobody was going to stop her.

Going to the tall broom closet, she reached for the mop. Wilton was pleading into the phone again. She realized with disgust it was another girl.

"When you gonna bend, baby? Don't you trust me?"

B.J. stole a look at her twenty-four-year-old brother slouched over the table fondling the receiver between his shoulder and cheek, a shit-kicking smile on his face. He was taller and thin, with blond hair cut almost in a military crew cut.

She hated her brother.

Wilton slammed the phone down and gave a hoot of laughter. Then he hiked his jeans up and watched his sister mop.

"Don't forget around the icebox. That's dirty."

B.J. said nothing as she methodically swished the mop around the ragged linoleum. Outside the kitchen she heard the melodic voice of an announcer in a commercial for Clairol Herbal Essence. Then she heard only Wilton.

"Saw you on Lake Road flirting with the boys," he said in his grating, singsong voice.

"I wasn't flirting. Those are my friends."

He laughed. "Friends don't want to do to you what they want to do."

B.J. swished the mop faster.

"Listen, baby sister, if anything like that happens to you, we'll just throw you out. You got a chance for a solid future and we want to give it to you."

Edward Bailey again. Why didn't they just wrap her up and deliver her to him? Then she frowned. They were trying to.

"You seem to be shacking up with every girl in Madison. Maybe I'll let them know about each other."

"It's different for me. I'm a man. And I support this family."

B.J. made a face.

"What are you? One of those women libbers? We ain't got no room for you around here."

B.J. groaned. She tuned him out, thinking again how it would look when she left. She'd wake up early in the morning if she slept at all. Then she'd hike up the long road to Madison itself. She wouldn't leave a note. By seven-thirty she would be on the bus heading for Cleveland. And some time that night she would be in the heart of glittering New York. So it didn't matter what he said. She lifted the pail and dumped it out on the other side of the sink; then she wrung the mop out. Wilton was still talking about Edward Bailey. Let *him* marry the man. She watched his twisted mouth, the arrogant expression on his face.

Suddenly she remembered the bathhouses near the old country club. She had always wondered how anyone could kill. God, how she would like to shut him up forever. He was always talking. He was always right. If she killed him, she would be free. Her grandparents couldn't do anything anymore.

Well, it was a nice fantasy. A new one. While he talked she imagined choking the breath out of him. Or taking a long kitchen knife and letting it rip apart his back.

She knew one thing. If he tried to stop her from going to New York and having a life for herself, she would kill him. Oh yes—she would. She'd kill anyone who tried to stand in her way.

Nobody could stop her now.

# Chapter Two

THE sound of the wheels on the gravel driveway acted as a doorbell. B.J. could see the drapes on the window in the front room pull back and then fall back into place. In seconds, Rachael Jorrish, clopping in mule house-slippers and holding the baby, appeared at the side of the car.

"Is that Josh?" B.J. squealed. She had baby-sat for whim when he was an infant of only four months. Now, when Rachael let him down, he took some steps hanging on to the bottom of her bermuda shorts.

As B.J. got out of the car and picked up the baby, Tom and Rachael exchanged looks. They hadn't seen B.J. since the end of last summer. Their baby-sitter had changed. She had become really gorgeous. Tom continued to gape at her until Rachael thumped him on the shoulder.

B.J., oblivious of the effect she had on people, spun around with the baby, who was giggling, enjoying the ride.

"Almost exactly thirteen months," Rachael said proudly.

"We had a birthday party for Mr. Chips," Tom said as they all went into the beautiful house.

"Why do you call him 'Mr. Chips'?" B.J. asked.

"Because we've been in the chips since he came," Rachael answered.

B.J. let Joshua down and watched him try to walk and then topple over. She stared down at him lovingly. Rachael and Tom Jorrish stared at her.

Then he cleared his throat. "I'd better close in the patio. There's a storm on the way."

"Oh dear," Rachael said. "I hope not. Joshie hates thunder."

B.J. put Joshie's little hand in hers and walked with him a few steps on the carpet. Then she picked him up. "He is so cute!" The baby seemed to appraise her. His hair was longish parted in front bangs, Buster Brown–style, except that his was a cap of golden curls surrounding large eyes. He kept working his mouth around a new tooth.

"We really should take him for a haircut soon," Rachael said, "but neither one of us has the heart to cut any of those little curls off."

B.J. noticed that the house hadn't changed much. The stairway leading to the second- and upper-level bedrooms was high-polished wood. The living room had tapestry hangings on the wall, two beige tweed couches and a wide chrome-and-glass coffee table. Off to the back was a patio where Mr. Jorrish was closing all the glass windows to keep out the coming shower. It was a beautiful summer home, B.J. thought, nicer than any of the Summers had. B.J. felt an ugly surge of envy she knew she'd never admit to.

When she made it, she would be rich. She would have all this. Just like the Jorrishes. She wanted to be just like the Jorrishes. But she wouldn't marry until after she was a star. If she married now, she would just be this girl from Madison, Ohio, who lived in a shack on Easton and Hall and was treated like the maid.

"B.J.," Rachael said. "Tell me, what is your secret?"

"Secret?" she said nervously. She thought of her plans to leave for New York the day after graduation.

"Yes, secret. I want to know how you changed like this. You're even more gorgeous this summer than you were last summer. As if someone waved a magic wand over you. If only we could bottle it. What did you eat?"

"Oh, the usual. Cheeseburgers, pizza, french fries."

Rachael laughed. They had wandered into her lovely bedroom. Joshie crawled steadily behind them.

"Rachael, dear, better start getting dressed," Tom Jorrish shouted. A boom of thunder ripped through the house and the loud noise made the baby cry. B.J. picked him up.

"So you just changed?" Rachael asked congenially.

"Something like that," B.J. said. She always felt a little shy with the Jorrishes. She had last year. It was a little better this year but she was more aware of her voice. She heard it like someone outside her body was talking for her.

"B.J., try this on later," Mrs. Jorrish said. She flung a powder-blue cowl-necked blouse with a blazer and skirt to match on the bed. "It's sure to fit you better than it does me. I think I gained a few pounds."

B.J. felt like asking where. Mrs. J. was gorgeous. She was a slim brunette with enormous brown eyes and a knock-'em-dead figure. She had skin that looked like ivory.

B.J. remembered to say "thank you" as more hangers with clothes fell onto the bed. Red jersey, shiny gold cloth, white linen. She might even wear one of these outfits on a TV show if she got lucky.

"Just need to run in and out of the shower. Keep an eye on Mr. Chips. He'll get into everything." Just as she said that, B.J. saw the baby at the pink-skirted vanity table. He was standing up on tiptoe and taking everything off of it—a pack of Virginia Slims, a Revlon

Formula II, and a lipstick that rolled across the carpet and under the bed.

B.J. retrieved it. Then she took his little wrist and shook it, saying, "No, no, no. Bad boy." He stared up into her face, studying her with those huge, brown velvety eyes.

She carried the baby into the living room and put him in his playpen, which was crowded with toys and stuffed animals of every size and color. The television was flickering to an empty room with a rerun of *M*A*S*H*.

"Can you zip me up, Beej?"

B.J. looked up. In came Rachael wearing a coral chiffon dress with a wide satin belt to match.

"Wow! Mrs. Jorrish, you look just great. Are you going dancing?"

"We're going to a new nightclub that just opened up outside of Ashtabula."

"Wow!" B.J. exclaimed again. Then she looked at Mrs. Jorrish's shoes and said "Wow!" again. She heard herself saying it, unable to take her eyes off the high-heeled spikes, silver, with dainty straps. They looked like something that had just come from an auction of MGM costumes.

"B.J., we can count on you for this summer, can't we?" she said. "We'll go home for about three weeks and then it's back out until September. Tom can continue to commute. Well, how about it, kid? You'll get a dollar raise on the hour. Well?"

"Well, um, you see," B.J. said, "it's like this. I'm going to New—New Hampshire to visit my aunt and uncle."

Rachael sat down on the couch like she had been dealt a blow. "Oh, how nice for you, B.J. But we'd like to have you in our little family. Maybe another raise in salary, you might reconsider?" Her voice was firm and persuasive, almost as if she knew she'd win.

24

B.J. shook her head and just said no again. All of the sudden, she wanted to confide her secret to Mrs. Jorrish. She of all people would have understood. But she couldn't tell her. She couldn't tell anyone. If anything went wrong, she wouldn't be able to leave Madison. Her brother would see to that. She would be stuck here the rest of her life. And if she didn't make it as an actress, she'd die.

"I have plenty of girlfriends who would jump at the idea of working for you, Mrs. Jorrish."

"I know. But I always want the best for my baby. And you're the best. You're steady and reliable and Joshie likes you. Even today, after nine months, he took to you and he doesn't get on with many strangers." She looked down and smiled. "I know you're thinking that I spoil him inordinately."

B.J. shook her head politely but they both knew she was lying.

"I spoil him, B.J., because I can't have any more children. Mr. Chips is it. He happened to us late in life and he's like this tiny miracle. I love him so much I ache with it."

"Well," said Tom Jorrish, coming into the room. "We're all dressed and ready to go." He kissed his wife. "You look beautiful, as always, Rachael. Is that the new dress?" B.J. felt her face turn warm and knew she was blushing. They were the perfect couple. They had everything in the world.

"Now, listen, B.J.," Rachael said. "Now that you're so grown-up and gorgeous-looking, you're going to have to take *wow!* out of your vocabulary. No cheeseburgers tonight. I fixed you a good dinner. It's in the oven. Just heat it to three-fifty. I wrote down two phone numbers. One is another couple who has a baby-sitter and the other is the number of the club. And don't answer the door to anyone."

"Oh no, B.J. Don't answer the door to anyone. We

heard there's been some trouble with a Peeping Tom in the neighborhood,'' Tom said. In his navy blazer and white pants with the red hankie sticking out of his pocket, Tom Jorrish looked a little like Robert Redford, she thought.

She carried the baby, who waved "bye bye" like an old pro, to the back door. Rachael blew him a kiss as the car backed noisily out of the gravel driveway.

B.J. closed the back door and locked it, trying to imagine the evening they would have. She couldn't picture what a fancy nightclub looked like. There were none in Madison.

The air was sticky and the mosquitos buzzed like whispering voices. It was going to rain any moment now and it wouldn't be a passing shower, she was sure of that. As she lifted the baby she saw a tree bend in the wind in the backyard. She wanted to put Joshie to bed before the storm started.

It was about eight-thirty and, as if he could tell the time, the baby began to wail on the bottom step. By the top step he was screeching so loud his little face was red and twisted up. B.J. put him in his crib, hoping he would just stop. Like the playpen, it was full of stuffed toys. She gave him a powder-blue teddy bear and he stopped crying to suck on an ear.

B.J. tiptoed out of the room and down the stairs, hoping he would just fall asleep before the thunder became deafening and the lightning illuminated the house with surprise attacks. The living room was sunken like in the movies. The carpeting was thick and deep, a lovely shade of burnt umber. She danced around in her sneakers and socks like she imagined they would at the nightclub. In the stove was a delicious dinner made especially for her. On the bed in the bedroom were several outfits she could try on and keep. For a few hours she could pretend she belonged here and that the Jorrishes were her real parents. She could be happy.

She wondered then if her mother had been a little like Rachael Jorrish. Grandmother wouldn't tell her. For some reason she hadn't liked her mother, the disapproval had always been obvious. Ever since B.J. was old enough to really understand what had happened, she had made up stories of what her life would have been like in Shaker Heights had her mother and father lived. It was a game she never tired of.

Because she felt cheated.

A crackle of lightning followed by a chorus of thunder reminded B.J. of a bowling alley. She put her fingers in her ears and when she took them out she heard the staccato screeching. The baby was up. She ran up the stairs two at a time.

The blue curtain was blowing with the breeze coming in through the open window. B.J. turned on the light and shut the window. Josh was clinging to a fuzzy pink stuffed poodle with a plastic rhinestone collar. His face was red and all scrunched up. It seemed like he was holding his breath and then he screamed louder.

B.J. reached down to pick him up as all his stuffed toys fell aside. "Poor Joshie," she cooed. "That was a loud and scary noise, wasn't it?" He put his little fingers on her mouth and his crying subsided. But he seemed to be trembling.

She took him downstairs and he became quiet.

"You just wanted to be held, didn't you, Joshua Jorrish?"

She put him on one of the beige couches. The yellow feet attached to his pajama legs were spread apart, the snaps unfastened. He wiggled around, trying to climb down from the couch.

B.J. picked him up and put him on the floor. Within seconds she was doubled over with laughter. Moving like a tiny feather duster, he swished across the floor, made it to the coffee table, and, buckling in his knees first, managed to stand straight up and reach the dish filled with multicolor hard candies. He stood straight up, grabbing a fistful.

"Whoa," B.J. cried.

She uncurled his little fist and took the candies away from him. He began to cry again. "Da-da," he said firmly.

Carrying Joshua into the kitchen, she looked out the window. It was streaked with rain and the lightning looked like a neon light painted over the dark. There was a deafening thunder clap and B.J. shivered. She hated thunderstorms.

She brushed the golden blond hair out of his eyes and took his thumb out of his mouth. He looked at her expectantly, waiting for something else to happen. She turned and walked up the steps. Almost on cue, he began to scream again.

That was followed by a flash of lightning so powerful it seemed to streak through the house. B.J. felt a little pinprick of fear. But all the doors were locked. And the windows were shut tight. A Peeping Tom. Oh well, it was probably some goofy kid from Madison High. That's all. It was just that this kind of dark, scary night made her feel so all alone. You never knew what was going to happen or what kind of damage it would do. Right now the waves on the lake were probably ten, twenty feet high. But she had always been afraid of rain at night.

Slick streets, driving, blinding rain, and death. Her parents had died in a rainstorm just like this.

Upstairs she put the baby back in his crib with all his colorful playmates. It was stuffy and humid. The baby's hair was matted damp across his forehead. B.J. went back to the window and opened it two inches, enough for a little breeze.

"Nightie night, Josh," she said.

B.J. was on the bottom step when she heard the insistent screams. She ran up the stairs two at a time and when the baby saw her he looked up, giggling. He was chewing on the tail of a black-and-white stuffed zebra.

B.J. loomed over the crib. "Joshua Jorrish. It's past your bedtime. Now, B.J. doesn't want to play. You have to go to bed."

Tiptoeing out of the room, she went downstairs thinking of the lovely dinner warming in the oven, of a phone call to her friend Debbie she wanted to make, and of all those designer clothes.

Almost at the bottom step, she heard the mournful squeaks that gave way to pitiful crying. Dashing back up the stairs, she rushed into his room. The minute he saw her, his face lit up, the tears stopped trickling down his face, and he smiled merrily showing her a nearly toothless little grin.

"Now listen up, Joshie," she said. "You can't do this all night. I won't have it."

The baby yawned.

"Good, you're tired. Now go to bed." She passed the open window and debated for a second whether to leave it open or close it. She lowered it about an inch.

When she got all the way down the steps she heard the piercing screams. Turning, exhausted, she looked up the stairs and shook her head. She knew what she'd find. He'd be laughing and want to play. He was just testing out what he thought was a new baby-sitter. The dumbest thing she could do would be to go upstairs. Nothing was wrong with Josh. She would be willing to bet her baby-sitting money on it.

It was the thunder and lightning and beating rain that made the baby's demands seem more important than they really were. So it took a lot of willpower to reach inside the refrigerator and not run up to look in on the baby again.

They had remembered. B.J. drank Coca-Cola. A lot of it. She poured herself a glass and dialed Debbie, who was baby-sitting nearer to the lake.

"Did you do all your math homework, yet?" Debbie asked her.

"Can't. The baby keeps crying. And then every time I go running up, he stops and starts to laugh. I'm going to let him cry."

"Let him be. Probably spoiled rotten," Debbie said. "God, this rain is driving me crazy. It must be the tail end of a hurricane. Do you wanna take the inner tubes and ride the waves tomorrow?"

"I can't."

Debbie knew better than to ask B.J. if her grandmother and obnoxious brother were keeping her busy.

"There's a Peeping Tom running around," B.J. said. The house seemed quiet and still.

"Keep the doors locked and close the drapes. All he can do is peep."

"I saw Hughie today," B.J. said brightly. "They're putting the cottage up for sale."

"Yeah," said Debbie. "It's over. We went and grew up and that's the end of us. I saw Barry. I was working a few hours waiting tables at the Bluebird. He was with a girl."

"What was she like?" B.J. asked. There was a time when everybody had a crush on Barry.

"She was very snooty. She had on this pantsuit and she kept clinging to Barry, saying, 'Baaaarrry.' I waited on their table and he introduced me as one of his friends. She gave me a funny look."

"Do you still like him?"

"The crush? Nah, it's over. He'll go to Northwestern this year and I'll go to Neubert's Beauty School in Painseville. Nah, I'm not his type."

There was a strip of lightning that lit up the sky as bright as day for just a second. Then B.J. heard the solid screeching of Josh. "My God, Deb, that baby is still crying. Maybe I should go up and just check."

"You'll only spoil him."

"Honestly, Debbie, I could kill that kid."

"Yeah, I know how you feel but don't let it get to you."

B.J. wanted so much to tell her secret to her friend. She would be the perfect person to tell. Just to say, I thought it over and I'm finally leaving. I'm going to New York. But she couldn't risk it. What if Debbie slipped and told Joyce and then Joyce told Linda, who had an older sister who for all she knew might be another of Wilton's girlfriends? And she'd be locked in her room until her wedding day to the smelly mortician and it would be her funeral and not her wedding.

She shuddered, remembering him.

He was gross.

She couldn't tell anyone, though she longed to. Where would she be without her friends? The kids had been everything to her for years.

An attack of thunder, a block of lightning, and B.J. saw a face pressing against the windowpane grinning. She shivered and then it was gone. Had it been there at all? Or had she imagined it.

Debbie was saying "Well, I can't tie up this phone. I'll see you Monday in school."

B.J. nodded. Her voice felt stuck in her throat. Seconds after she hung up, the lights went out. But it was just for a second. Then they came on again.

B.J. felt like calling back her closest friend and screaming, *I'm stuck way out here alone and I'm scared. Talk to me just a little while longer.*

I'm terrified of the storm.

Just like I was when we were little, remember?

She stared at the phone and all the lights all over the house went out again. Carefully feeling around with her hands, panicked, she grabbed a pack of matches. Lighting one, she tried, from the tiny glow, to make her way closer to the cabinet where there might be some candles. She wondered if they kept them there or even if they had any.

Upstairs the baby was screaming.

She looked at the dark, vast space where the steps would be. It was black in the house except for little spurts of light coming from the lightning.

She lit match after match, burning her fingertips, but she couldn't find any candles. Upstairs the baby had started to screech. And lightning framed a face in the window. Or was she imagining it? Holding her breath, she almost screamed when she heard the doorbell ringing.

# Chapter Three

THE doorbell was ringing incessantly. Crying softly, she waited until the noise stopped. Maybe that was the Peeping Tom. Maybe he was really a rapist and a killer. She knew the doors and windows were shut and locked, but she wanted to run and double-check.

Then the lights came on again.

Without thinking, she ran up the steps taking them two at a time, seizing onto the railings. The baby was asleep finally.

She stood in the doorway of the little room that had been painted powder blue. Mobiles hung from the ceiling down to his crib. One of pink and green elephants and another of polka-dotted clowns. They dangled and danced in the breeze, lit by the soft glow of the night-light.

The baby was sleeping soundly. He must have knocked himself out with all that crying.

Then B.J. noticed the window. It was closed, just the way she had left it. The rain had been hard driving and might have come into the room. She looked over the room once again. The little tables and chairs were dry. There was a pile of toys in the corner, stuff that was waiting for him to grow into—a catcher's mitt and a football. In the corner was a huge yellow-and-brown stuffed giraffe. It was probably bigger than the baby.

B.J. smiled at the baby sleeping soundly. She had pictured having a screeching baby on her hands all night. She tiptoed over. The blanket was up to his neck. His long eyelashes fanned his face like a little girl's.

She wanted to rest a bit, have that chicken dinner, and try on all those lovely clothes that would be hers. The worst part of the storm had to be over.

But when she got to the bottom step she shook her head.

Something was wrong. The old expression popped into her head: "Can you see anything wrong with this picture?"

The window. She hadn't ever closed the window. It was left open—only two inches, but it was still open. She ran up the stairs. She knew the thirteen-month-old baby didn't slip out of his crib and close it. Maybe it had slipped in the wind.

Hands trembling, she was remembering the jeering face at the window. She had seen him and then within seconds the face was gone.

Quickly she snapped around, feeling someone staring at her in the doorway. But it was no one. Then she remembered the insistent doorbell. Someone had been here.

Her mouth fell open and she jumped a little when a loud, almost angry clap of thunder shattered the silence of the little room. B.J. put her fingers in her ears, feeling her heart pounding. Hadn't Mr. Jorrish said the baby hated the sound of thunder? But he hadn't woke up, hadn't moved.

B.J. studied his pretty little face. It was too quiet in the room. She wanted him to wake up, she wanted to hold him and play with him. She just wanted some company to help her get through the night. She was scared to be alone in the storm with the lights going off

34

and on and the doorbell ringing. She could always put him to bed again.

At the bottom of it all, she had this sickening feeling that something was wrong, very, very wrong.

"Wake up, Joshie," she said in a tiny voice. "Wake up, it's time to play. You can scream all you want." She knew what she was doing was insane but she couldn't stop herself.

The baby didn't move.

"Wake up, Joshie," she said in a tiny voice. "Scream all you want."

The baby didn't move.

"Damn you, baby, wake up!"

With tears streaming down her face, knowing she was scared and out of control, she picked the baby up. His head wobbled and then crashed on her shoulder. She felt his weight against her. The baby felt heavy, droopy somehow. Maybe he needed his diaper changed. She patted his little back.

Maybe she had shut the window and forgotten about it. She was sure she was being silly. Waking up the baby would be inviting trouble. As she went to put him back in his crib, she noticed she was handling him like a newborn infant.

She noticed something else: The baby had stopped breathing.

Then she screamed again, "Wake up! Damn you, wake up!" She threw him in his crib, raced down the steps, and picked up the phone. There was no sound.

The phone was dead.

She shut her eyes.

And the baby was dead.

Running up the stairs, taking them three at a time, she picked up the baby. There was such a stillness. She opened one of his eyes and it stayed that way, a glassy brown eye like a searchlight. Then she dropped him in his crib and shut the eye. The window. That's how it

35

had happened. Someone had come in through the window somehow. That's why the window was shut.

She smelled fire. Running down the steps again, tripping down the last three, she looked around the kitchen. Something was burning. She turned up her nose trying to figure out what it was, thinking of the dead baby upstairs.

Then she remembered her dinner. That chicken. It seemed so nice, then. How she longed to turn back the clock. Just take the hands and force them back in time.

She sat on the cold linoleum floor cross-legged, trying to figure it out. Rocking, she knew a killer had been in the house. Hugging herself, she wondered if the killer was still there. Hiding in the basement? Lurking in the attic?

She ran to the door and looked across the grounds. It was raining hard. Maybe she could pretend it hadn't happened. Maybe she should call someone.

Maybe she was wrong.

She had to be wrong. How could anything like that happen? Stuff like that happened to other people, didn't it?

Tired, aching, half out of her mind, B.J. dragged up the steps again. She stood by the crib and stared at little Joshua Jorrish. He looked like he was sound asleep at first.

Then you noticed the stillness, the quietude, as if he had changed into a tiny marble statue.

"Oh no, oh my God, why?" she screamed, rocking back and forth. Why couldn't it have been a nightmare? Someone had snuck in while she was downstairs and murdered this perfect little baby. Someone had broken in and snuffed out the life of this little baby. Had snuffed out the life of this innocent child.

A dead baby.

She stared at it. It was so grotesque it was hard to

believe. One minute he had been crying and laughing and now he was dead. He would never grow up.

She put her hands to her face. She couldn't cry. And she ached painfully to sob. Running to the window, she placed her hands on the sill and looked at the inky, wet night. Someone had come up and killed Joshie. Little zigzags of lightning laced the sky, and like a jolt of electric current she could feel her sanity beginning to return.

In the distance she could make out the ravine. The killer might still be nearby, might be hiding there. Then she remembered the quick jerks of the doorbell. Had that been someone wanting to come in, wanting to kill her?

She looked down tenderly at Joshie. She tucked him in and gave him one of his sweet, soft toys. For a second she slipped into the welcoming oblivion of the insane, telling herself she had just imagined it. How could it be true?

Another sharp crackle of thunder followed by a ragged line of lightning made her jump. She ran downstairs. Vaguely aware of her stomach rumbling, she reached into the candy dish and grabbed a handful of candy. Then she remembered the little china doll-like baby with the head that rolled back and she screamed and dropped the candy.

She ran into the kitchen and spotted a long, sharp knife. Without thinking, she snatched it up and ran outside.

The killer was outside; she felt it. She was going to kill him before he killed her. The rain was still falling in torrents. Her sneakers sunk into the muddy grass. Swallowing hard, lifting the knife and jabbing into the wet night, she ran across the enormous backyard.

There was a wide streak of lightning, so thick it lit up the whole yard and for a minute it looked like someone had turned on the lights. Even without the lightning to light her way, she could see. Someone was there, somewhere.

There was a hideous scream and it took a moment to realize the ugly noise was coming from inside her. Then the rain began again even harder; she felt it washing over her face, like the tears that wouldn't come.

Stumbling in the mud, she scrambled to regain her balance. She knew her shoelaces were untied but she didn't care. She kept running, remembering the Joshie of just four hours ago. The fair hair, the sparkling eyes, the bright little smile. Up ahead by the ravine, she thought she saw something. A dark figure in the dark night, silhouetted in the moonlight.

Sobbing, she raised her knife.

"Stop! Stop you!" she yelled as the figure leaped away, dancing in and out of the flashes of lightning like some dark gargoyle. B.J. was out of breath now, her lungs aching and her breath coming in heavy gasps like sobs.

"Stop! You!" she yelled again. She was closer now, close enough to see him when he turned. The sky lit up again with a bolt of lightning and provided her with a full view. She saw a man with black, curly hair. Raising her knife, she let out a cry and ran, tripping and falling in the mud. But it was no good. The man had run away and she couldn't see him anymore. Her clothes had become transparent and seemed painted on her. Her hair hung sopping wet in her eyes and her sneakers were like little tubs of water. She had dropped her knife somewhere.

But she had seen him. The killer. Shuddering, she walked back. He had disappeared. But they would catch him.

When she came back into the house nothing had changed. Joshie was upstairs in his little crib with all of his fine toys. And then she recalled way back when

38

she was three and her mama and daddy were in those big boxes. She was just a pumpkin-colored little girl all dressed up in a new dress as she tried to kiss her mama. She shivered. She knew she was cold and wet and hungry. She also knew her clothes were muddy. She sat in the middle of the kitchen and sang in a high, squeaky voice, "Humpty Dumpty sat on a wall, Humpty Dumpty had a great fall."

Then she stopped and put her hands over her ears to shut out her whiny singing. There was something she had to do. She had forgotten.

Elmo. She shut her eyes and prayed. Dear God, let the phone not be dead like the baby and the chicken. Elmo. She had to hear his voice. And then miracuously the phone was ringing and someone picked up on the second ring.

"Elmo, it's you!" she shouted.

There was a silence.

"Elmo, it's B.J."

"Beej, how's everything," the police office said. "Why are you calling us? Anything wrong? Are your grandparents, okay?"

"Elmo, I'm in trouble. I'm baby-sitting for the Jorrishes and they're from Shaker Heights and Elmo—"

"Listen, B.J., spare the high-school theatrics. Do you know how many crank calls like this I have gotten from your graduating class this month? They all baby-sit and they all dial old Elmo!"

"Elmo, there's a dead baby here!" B.J. screeched and then sobbed to hear herself say it. "Oh, God, I wish it were a prank. Oh, Elmo, a dead baby. Someone came in, I think, through the upstairs window and murdered that little baby right here."

She could hear him sighing. Her hands were trembling. Twice she had had to dial the number of the Madison Police Force. Finally he said, "Give me the address, B.J."

Her mind went blank. She didn't know the address, only that there was gravel in the back and that it was the only lavender-shuddered house in all of Madison.

"Just the facts, now, B.J. And let's get this thing settled."

"The old Nixon property, right behind the theater. And Elmo, hurry. Someone wanted to kill that baby and that someone might be waiting. I ran out to the ravine and that's where I saw him. He was lit up like an electric sign and he laughed at me and ran away. I dropped my knife somewhere in the rain. Oh, God, I'm so scared Elmo."

Her teeth were chattering.

"Where's the baby?"

"In his crib," B.J. said defensively.

"Okay, Beej, now don't touch anything. Least of all the baby. Now give me some more address. Where is it?"

"Where's what!"

"B.J., don't talk crazy. Not now. Or I can't help you. Give me some directions."

"Behind the Rabbit Run Theatre. There's a little fork in the road. Turn to the right—I mean the left—and there's gravel in the driveway that scrunches like Cheerios." She started to screech hysterically. "Oh God, please don't leave me alone with that dead baby. Wait until the Jorrishes find out. Oh, God, sweet Jesus, everyone will think I killed little Joshie."

"Listen up, B.J." Elmo had a funny feeling he didn't like. "Again, don't touch anything. Oh God, your fingerprints must be all over. And the baby?"

"Well, I've been touching him all night, even while he was living I— Just please come!"

"Hang loose, Beej. And if they have any booze better have a swig now."

"Elmo," a teeny voice asked. "What's going to happen to me?"

40

"Shhhh. Listen, I don't know. If there's a dead baby, we call in the Painseville police. That's the county seat. You know Madison's just a one-horse town."

B.J. didn't reply. For ten merciful minutes, she had fallen asleep.

At the Pink Pussycat in Ashtabula, Tom was dancing tight with his friend's wife. At the moment he couldn't remember her name. Big tits though. He could see Rachael was glued to the other husband. Who knew? Maybe they'd end up together. It helped their marriage to have a little innocent affair together rather than separately. Sometimes he suspected Rachael didn't like it as much as she claimed she did. God, were they drunk.

"Wanna have some fun?" Tom said. "We got this gorgeous kid for a baby-sitter. Let's call her up. I mean, she looks like a teenage movie star. I mean, last year she was just this pretty little girl, now she would rival Sophia Loren."

The other man could feel an erection starting. Baby-sitters excited him. The younger the better. "Oh, I don't think we should," Rachael said. "Although we should check on the baby." She laughed and looked at the other three. "Okay, but just for a few minutes. We don't want to scare her. And then put me on."

B.J. was rocking on the steps, pretending he was still alive, with a pain in her stomach that was as sharp as eating too many candied apples.

The phone rang and she wimpered. She thought she would go crazy if Elmo didn't get there immediately.

"Hello?"

"Hi, gorgeous. I like baby-sitters and I heard you're a knockout, so tell me all about it."

"Who is this?" she cried. She felt crazy. This was the killer. It had to be.

She started to sob and then she heard the soothing

41

voice of Rachael. "Oh, B.J., did that man scare you? Now just hush because everything's okay. Just some crazy, drunken fools. How's the baby? Did our Mr. Chips run you ragged?"

There was silence on the other end.

"Well, is my darling sleeping?"

Oh God, where was Elmo?

"B.J., is anything wrong?"

She didn't know what to say. And she couldn't stop the sobs, the loud racking sobs.

Suddenly Rachael sobered up. "Tom, I think we should leave."

"Leave so early, why?"

Rachael had a funny, ugly feeling in her stomach. The baby was sick and she wasn't telling. And she sounded so—so not like sweet B.J.

And then she hung up on them.

"Elmo," she sobbed as she heard his car on the gravel driveway outside.

# Chapter Four

"Where's the baby, B.J.?" Elmo said.

Her eyes were vacant-looking and she looked like she could use a bath.

"The killer, Elmo. Don't just stand there. Find the killer."

Her beautiful hair was hanging, limp, in her eyes, which seemed dark, like they had no pupils. Silently he prayed he was wrong.

Elmo Hopper was tall and always shy of about twenty pounds. When he had turned thirty, his hair had turned gray and graduated to a snow white. He reminded B.J. of Santa Claus. Suddenly her face changed and she broke into a smile. Elmo was here. He would find the killer in the ravine and then everything would be okay and she could leave on that bus and go to New York and make it. After graduation.

"Where's the baby, B.J.?"

"Upstairs," B.J. whispered. Talking hurt her throat. "He's in his little room with all his stuffed animals." She began to cry.

"Okay, you stay here. Sit down and try to calm down." As he took the mahogany steps, Elmo saw he was going two at a time. He found himself praying that this was one of B.J.'s cuckoo, kooky schemes or pranks.

He wouldn't even reprimand her. God, he remembered when her parents had been killed on the highway. And her grandparents and that brother of hers. No, it hadn't been easy for B.J. Maybe she should get married and get out of the house.

He crossed himself and went into the baby's room with its look of a toy store. In the center of the room was a crib with mobiles. In the center was a beautiful little blond-haired baby. No problem with fingerprints, B.J. had already touched them. There was no pulse. The baby was dead.

He picked it up and watched with terror as his head fell back or to the front like it was a little marionette. Then he walked down the steps slowly. B.J. sat, a lone figure in the big couch. Unaware that her clothes were wet and muddy, she just sat in the middle of the cream-colored couch looking small and helpless. "Elmo, the killer! I wouldn't kill that baby. Look for the killer. And the window, Elmo, I closed the window and then it was open. You're looking for someone who placed a ladder under the window."

He marveled at how sane she seemed. But there was nothing he could do. Just remove her to Painseville and out of the way; then Madison and Painseville could investigate. Sooner or later the parents would come.

"You don't believe me," she said suddenly, horrified. "You think I killed that baby."

He sat and stroked her arm in little circles. Maybe there was a killer. He knew B.J. wouldn't kill a baby. His heart ached for the young couple and for this young girl. He could only imagine trying to find this killer who was no doubt nowhere nearby.

"Look, Beej, I'll help you as much as I can but you know that you're in a lot of trouble."

Together they waited for the gravel, the sound of the car pulling up and gliding over the pebbles. Then the quiet as it stopped.

B.J. put her head in her hands and then lifted it as Rachael and Tom walked into the room.

"What are you doing here?" Rachael demanded of Elmo Hopper.

"Is the baby sick? I saw your car parked outside. You know B.J. can't have any visitors."

"It's the Peeping Tom, that's all Rachael," Tom said.

Then they stared at the wild-eyed B.J. sitting in her wet, muddy, clothes, ruining the couch. It was Rachael who caught it first. She ran into the kitchen, turned the stove off and stared at the black charcoal chicken. A few minutes longer and there might have been a fire.

"What the hell is going on here, officer?" she shouted, coming into the living room. She glared at B.J. "Okay, something's wrong with the baby?" She turned and clattered up the steps in her silver high-heeled shoes with her husband following. Elmo was silent. There was nothing he could say until . . .

Then they heard the horrible, high-pitched scream. Elmo sighed. Now it was beginning.

B.J. pleaded with him. "Let me stay in the Madison jail for just tonight. I can't go back to Grandmother. They just won't understand. They'll probably think I did it!"

Then they saw Rachael, hardly able to walk, her beautiful dress twisted around her waist, wobbling down the steps with Tom trying to hold her up. She was carrying her baby, cuddling him as if he were still alive.

Tom Jorrish looked at Elmo and said, "Get her out of here. Call whoever you have to and have her arrested."

Rachael was smiling sweetly, holding Mr. Chips.

"You can't stay here, Mr. Jorrish," Elmo said. "Pretty soon forensics specialists will be here from Painseville. I just have to call them now."

Tom pointed to the phone in the kitchen. Elmo took

some paper towels and put his hand on the phone. "Can you go to Cleveland tonight?" he asked the couple. There was no answer.

He quickly did what he had to. As expected, Painseville was surprised. Nothing ever happened in Madison.

He came back into the room. Tom, ashen-faced, was watching his wife trying to give Joshie a little bottle of orange juice as it drooled down his face.

Elmo was trying to figure out how to do this delicately, when B.J. screamed. "A killer killed that baby! The window was closed and then it was open. Someone came up a ladder and killed him!"

Tom shook his head. "Why would anyone want to kill our baby? Kidnapping I could understand, but this . . ." He looked at Elmo. "Just get her out of here, before I kill her . . . slowly."

"Mr. Jorrish, I just called Painseville and they will send a car. She will be transferred to the Painseville jail to await a pretrial."

"No," B.J. said. "No, you don't understand it. I didn't do it."

"B.J.," Elmo said sternly, "if you don't just sit on that there couch and say nothing, I'll make you sit in the squad car alone in the rain. Now, we'll tell you what to do. And when we do, you will do it. There's a dead baby here, B.J., and so far we have no evidence that you weren't responsible."

Rachael was reading to Joshie about Babar the Elephant, one of his favorites, but he wasn't responding to Rachael's admonishment. "Sit up."

"I really think you should check into a motel tonight and then you should see about getting your wife medical attention."

Then Tom burst into tears, unashamedly. B.J. had never seen a man cry. "God, just a few hours ago he was . . . I can't believe it. Put down the baby, Rachie. Come with me, yes?''

But Rachael was reading to the baby, protecting him from strange hands.

B.J. closed her eyes, smiling dreamily. If only she could go back in time and freeze there. She felt she was going crazy. Nobody believed her.

Rachael's cheerful reading continued as she pointed out the elephant to her baby. Elmo's heart went out to this man trying so desperately to keep himself together with no support from his sick wife.

''The baby should be taken to the Painseville morgue.''

Suddenly Rachael Jorrish said, ''No, Joshie's coming with us back to Cleveland. As soon as he wakes up.''

For some reason Elmo thought to look at B.J. She was eating the flowers from the vase on the coffee table.

Tom went over and hugged his wife but refused to touch the dead baby. If he did, he would be sick to his stomach and they needed him to be strong.

He took a swig of scotch right from the bottle. Then he looked at the not-so-gorgeous baby-sitter. Now she was ugly.

Somehow Tom and Elmo pried the baby from Rachael, who kept showering it with kisses. It.

''How do they do this . . .''

''Just put him in his crib and the Painseville Police Force will take care of the rest.''

Tom retreated to the bar and took another swig. That's when he saw the baby-sitter with flowers falling out of her mouth. His son looked like a glassy-eyed doll. His wife's mind had snapped in the shock of it all. And the now-not-so-gorgeous baby-sitter looked and behaved like what the sixties used to call a flower child.

He then took the baby from Elmo and took it upstairs, crying all the way.

Elmo was looking at B.J. chomping on the little leaves they put behind those flower bouquets.

"Can she have a little glass of milk or something?" Elmo asked Rachael.

"Milk? Give her hemlock."

And she got up and ran up the steps to protect her baby.

WHEN the doorbell rang, Elmo said, "That was fast."

It was one in the morning and the rain had tapered off but it was still showering. Rachael burst into fresh tears. "I'm not leaving him with these strangers. It's not kind, you see and I . . ."

It was Elmo who started to crack under the stress.

"Oh, c'mon, you guys are like bloodsuckers." But, in fact, they were just doing their job.

"It's not the police. Just the press." By way of apology, Elmo said, "I'll get rid of them." Then he turned to two guys, one with a felt hat on and the other with a yellow slicker and said, "Have a heart. Tomorrow, they'll talk tomorrow."

But they already had one foot in the door. B.J. had drowsed a bit and when she woke up, she thought she saw a flashlight. Then she realized it was a flashbulb. They had shot her at a bad moment. God, she almost looked pleased. But she discovered that if she shut her eyes and slept, the weight didn't sit on her heart pressing whatever button that would make her cry again.

Elmo was just pushing them out the door when Rachael, standing near her husband, hands on hips, elbows out, cried, "No, stay. I'll tell you the story. Anything that will give us our justice."

The reporters took out their pads. One flicked a tape recorder on.

"She killed him," Rachael said. "She was here alone with him. She killed him."

The other reporter whistled low and his partner knew

48

what he meant. Gorgeous B.J., slightly daft for years, finally made a real boo-boo.

"No, I didn't," B.J. shouted. "There was a killer!"

"Okay, you guys, you got to get out of here. Come back later, okay?"

This was the kind of pretrial publicity B.J. didn't need, he thought, and the reporters knew it. It wasn't fair. Not in a one-horse town.

Tom sensed the volcanic situation and gripped his wife around the shoulder. "C'mon, honey, you want this in the Cleveland papers? Let's go to a motel now and get some rest."

But they had already been kicked out the door. "Do you have a search warrant, Elm?" one said sarcastically.

B.J. looked around the room and started to cry again, then said steadily, "No, you don't understand. The window was closed and then it was open and I didn't leave it that way and then I realized a killer had come into the house and I ran with one of the kitchen knives to the ravine and some lightning . . ." She stopped to take another breath of air. Both Tom and Rachael were moderate smokers who were chain-smoking. A little cloud of smoke hung over the room.

After they were kicked out, one reporter said, "What about 'Beautiful Baby-sitter Turns Baby Killer'?"

Inside, Elmo was saying, "Since Painseville should be here any minute, can I just ask you folks to hang around a few minutes longer? The detectives will want to ask you just a few questions."

"A Valium," she said, like she had to go to the bathroom, which was also true. "Just one. I can't stand it."

The doorbell again and B.J. stopped what she was doing—tearing the cellophane off the sour-ball candies, chewing them halfway, then putting the candy back in the dish. The chrome-and-glass clock was heading toward two in the morning.

She looked up. The couple weren't police. Elmo studied the floor. Shit. He had made a big mistake. Mary and John Stronger didn't say hello, they just plowed in, the old man depending on his walker. Her grandmother was now on a cane for some ailment or other.

They were a noble sight.

"You put on one radio and Christ Almighty it gets played all over town," her grandmother said. "Everyone knows about your little escapade, B.J. Just so you know you won't get any help from us. We don't have the money and we—"

"Believe you did it," her grandfather finished.

B.J. let out a loud sigh.

"You'll get nothing from us. So don't wait. Make your own arrangements."

Elmo shook his head.

Mercifully, the Painseville police pulled up over the driveway onto the grass. There were already too many cars in the gravelly driveway. The reporters got a glimpse of them and a flash or two went off.

"Jail," B.J. said, as if she were trying the word on for size.

Her grandmother shook her walking stick at B.J. "Always knew she was bad from the day we got her. We'll do nothing for you, missy. No help. Now we have a house of shame."

Elmo rubbed his forehead. The Strongers—just what they needed now. He tried to shoo them out but they wouldn't go. "Jail," B.J. said again, still grappling with the word like a three-year-old. She couldn't figure it out. Why couldn't she go to the Madison Lockup and play gin rummy until they found the killer? In fact, why weren't they looking for him now? She would never forget the ugly, laughing face near the ravine. She didn't do it. But she was the only one who believed that.

Painseville. Her only memory of Painseville was when she and Debbie had borrowed her dad's car and driven there to shop. Debbie had bought a new white blouse but B.J.'s money was tied up for her departure so she didn't feel deprived. She made a show of not liking anything. They had stopped at Woolworths and ordered cokes and cheeseburgers and gossiped about all the kids.

Two detectives and a woman walked in and shook hands with Elmo. It was about three in the morning but B.J. knew she'd never sleep. She'd never sleep again until they found the murderer.

"I'm Detective Simmons, Painseville," he said to Tom Jorrish. There was a commotion outside and Elmo shrugged, elbows in, hands out. They had their TV cameras. She'd probably be in the news. Madison didn't have their own TV station, but Mentor and Painseville and Ashtabula did.

"This will just take a minute, ma'am," he said respectfully to Mrs. Jorrish.

The Valium wasn't working. She needed something stronger. Maybe a Benedryl. "My son, he's upstairs."

"How did you pick this girl to be your baby-sitter? Did you know anything about her life?"

Rachael stared at this man.

"Do you need to know?" asked Tom.

"Yes, sir, we do."

"We advertised for her on a bulletin board in the general store. That little store on the lake. We didn't know we'd get some psycho case. Boy, I wish we had picked someone else," Tom said softly.

B.J. noticed that no one asked her anything. The voices gave orders and they were harsh and disgusted-sounding. No one let her speak. If they would, she'd tell them about the window and the ladder and the real

51

killer. There was a real killer, wasn't there? She slept or dozed.

"I'll need your name and address," Simmons said as he flashed his gold shield at the Jorrishes.

The other detectives would remain through the night with Elmo handling the forensics.

Rachael cried out. "Please, something, another Valium. I feel like I'm jumping out of my skin."

Tom handed the detectives his business card. Try as he might, he couldn't remember their address in Shaker Heights.

"Oh, please don't take my little treasure to that cold place, the morgue. Surely you wouldn't let your child play there."

The detective looked at Elmo as if to say, We've got a bunch of loonies on our hands.

The matron shot a mean look at B.J. "Why are you sitting in that muddy raincoat on this nice couch? You've ruined it. Bad girl."

B.J. knew one thing. This woman could teach Grandmother some new tricks. B.J. was being treated as though she were crazy. The Jorrishes were talking quietly to the detectives and the forensics experts were already upstairs photographing and getting fibers and hair off the baby with a tiny vacuum cleaner.

Simmons found baby murders especially obnoxious. Though he didn't want to be judgmental, he knew the kid had done it. Why? Because she was a poor little girl and she was envious. Basically that and then God knows what else the shrinks would find.

He had seen a lot. First in New York City and then in his important job here. Painseville wasn't all that bad. He took the job seriously. After his wife had gone through the umpteenth miscarriage, she had wanted to return to small-town living. Three children later, he realized he had made a mistake. But it was too late in the game to go back. He photographed and marveled at what a beautiful little baby. Joshua. Josh. Dead now. He pitied the parents. Simmons had almost named his son Joshua.

The killer. His men had staked out the killer but it had rained hard. There was not a shred of evidence to hang anything on. No footprints, no fingerprints except hers, no sign of a ladder, all markings washed away, a knife with no trace of blood, and an eccentric but gorgeous little baby-sitter.

Downstairs Tom was literally pulling his wife out of the house. "Joshie—we can't leave him alone, darling. He's never been alone."

Maybe it was better that they stay in a motel, Tom thought. God knew, he was in no shape to drive himself. But they had to get out of their house. Maybe if he made just one more check, Joshie might still be alive and in a coma. He started upstairs.

The downstairs detective stood blocking him at the base of the steps. "Excuse me, sir, where are you going?"

"To the bathroom."

"I believe there's one off the kitchen, sir."

"Can't I have one more look at our boy? He was such a cute little guy."

Elmo made sure he was clearing the house of anybody who didn't belong in it and he noted the irony of kicking the owners out. The detectives would notify them. The morgue would release the body in a day or two.

It was obvious they didn't want to leave. The poor mother was hardly able to stand.

B.J. watched it all and saw herself walking up that road with her suitcases around about dawn, flagging down that bus that would take her through Cleveland and on to New York City. Because if she didn't think of that as reality and the present moment as fantasy she would go out of her head. Funny, now she saw herself

53

as others must have. The loony, kookie, but beautiful
B.J. so all is forgiven. Except she didn't sense that anyone was forgiving her tonight. Later they'd be sorry.

One officer put her wrists into handcuffs.

Even Elmo winced. "Oh, did you have to do that?
She's only sixteen."

She wanted to correct him. She was seventeen and
due to graduate in a month from Madison High. Suddenly she saw her life pouring through her fingers like
sand on the beach. She started to scream and the officer
smacked her across the face. "Don't like tantrums, girl.
Save that for your trial. Looks like you're going to need
it."

Outside, the photographers and reporters were waiting for this knockout kid who had murdered these rich
folks' baby. It was maybe the first good copy they'd
seen in decades. Some had never seen something as big
as this. They weren't going to waste a moment to cover
this story to its fullest.

# Chapter Five

Iт had started to rain again and B.J. didn't know where her tears started and the rain left off. A police matron, a fat, burly woman with hair on her chin, kept chain-smoking. The detective returning to Painseville drove them. Sitting in the front seat alone like a chauffeur, he kept adjusting the rearview mirror in order to get a better look at her. She was gorgeous, a face like a movie star, and a body to match. How could someone with her whole future ahead of her do it?

Then he reminded himself who he was. Just a second-grade dick from a town nobody remembered and who most folks didn't know about anyhow. But when this hit the papers, they might mention his name. His wife would appreciate that. He wanted to feel sorry for her because she was just a kid but he couldn't forget the image of the poor mother and father. His daughter was expecting anyday now.

It was somewhere between five and six, around dawn, B.J. figured. Her two hands ached because they were shackled so closely to each other and it seemed like her arms and wrists had hurt like that until they went numb. She couldn't figure out which was the better of the two.

She knew she felt a raw, nagging hunger in her stomach. She couldn't take the smoke of the chain-smoking matron next to her. Every time she would doze off, the matron would nudge her. B.J. figured she was supposed to stay awake, for some reason. If she could sleep she would pretend nothing existed and that this had never happened to her.

The driver switched on the radio to keep awake.

"And this just in from Madison, Ohio. A young teenager, B.J. Stronger, age seventeen, a local girl, is heading toward the Painesville jail this morning. She is the alleged killer of a thirteenth-month-old baby at a baby-sitting job. And now let's have a weather—"

Another microphoned voice. Another announcer giving the weather and a traffic dispatch. Morning. B.J. thought of toast she could dunk in regular coffee. Maybe an egg. Or some bran muffins. At least some orange juice.

Then the announcer came on again and she wished she could block her ears.

"More about that baby-sitting killing over there on Madison-on-the-Lake. The parents of that beautiful blue-eyed blond child will not comment on the events. They are from Shaker Heights. The alleged suspect, B.J. Stronger, is from right here on the lake. She was— is—supposed to graduate from Madison High. Stay tuned for more on this sensational case."

B.J. stared at the window, saying nothing.

The driver continued to look at her.

The matron had pulled out a roast-beef hero and was noisly eating it. B.J.'s stomach rumbled. No one had spoken a word out loud since they got in the car. Suddenly she felt a pang of terror running up her spine.

ELMO and the Madison police force, which consisted of a nearly retired officer and a secretary of about sixty or so, assisted the forensic team as best they could. None of them really believed B.J. was as daffy as the news reports say she had a reputation to be. Most of them knew the family one way or another.

God, Elmo had prayed as they entered the tool shed, please find a wet, rain-glossy ladder. But they hadn't found anything that might be interpreted as incriminating evidence.

B.J. said she saw a man—she'd described him—and then he got away. Then she took a knife and went after him but dropped it.

One of the detectives ordered a search of the ravine for the ladder or the man. "We can't rely on the usual signs, I'm afraid. The rain took care of that."

"Damn fucker," said one of the detectives.

"The man who got away?" Elmo asked hopefully.

"Uh, no, Sergeant, I was thinking of that little thundershower we had. It all but washed away any evidence to support that a man was on the premises."

They had found no prints around the rim of the upstairs window. It was close to six and the lovely summer home looked like a crime scene. The Painseville morgue had come at four and they watched as the man, confused, searched for a tiny body bag.

"No one told me it was a baby," he said on the defensive.

Finally he sighed and somehow rolled one into three parts.

Soon Joshua Jorrish's curly hair disappeared into the black bag. But he had long since stopped resembling a baby. Rigor mortis had set in and he looked like a corpse, a small corpse.

Elmo looked down as the van pulled off, headed toward Painseville. He wondered about B.J. It had broken his heart when he saw her handcuffed like that. John and Betty Jo's daughter. It hurt him so. She shouldn't have been with her grandparents. A foster home of strangers would have been kinder. Also, something kept bugging him all night. There literally wasn't a shred of evidence to support her premise.

Reporters were now swarming through the place as if it were a giant anthill.

He knew he would be assaulted and he didn't want to talk to the press in his frame of mind. Exhausted, angry, frustrated—to name a few of the emotions. As his wife would say, "Get something in your stomach, El, and you'll be just fine."

He had been hungry before. Now he had lost his appetite.

He tried as best he could to avoid them as he walked toward his car.

"Hey, Elmo," said someone from the *Madison Free Press*.

"Is it true she was nutty as a fruitcake?"

He inhaled and got a sharp pain in his gut. He had trained himself over the years to stop his fist from ramming someone in the jaw.

"She had an unhappy home life, that was all. And a vivid imagination."

"Are you saying you think she is innocent?"

"I ain't saying nothing. But you boys know the name of the game. No comment."

But the reporters were hungry for every word. A gorgeous teenager raised so strictly, and with her looks. It was a dream assignment and a thankless job for anyone trying to protect her.

"We just went over to her friend's house, Debbie Newsom."

"What did she say?" Elmo's back was to them. Without a word, he got in his car.

"Her mother came to the door. Said she had no comment."

THE sedative had arrived with the local doctor. "I'm just going to give you Dalmane," the old physician

58

said. "It's just a nonbarbituate sleeping pill. Just something to tide you over until you get to your internist in Cleveland. Terrible thing about B.J. Such a pretty girl. Must be a mistake. Well, we have some time to see if it was a mistake."

They were in a Holiday Inn on Route 20. The doctor had come around three o'clock, roused out of his bed and eager to help them.

Rachael, shaking and gray-faced, sat on one of the two blue chenille bedspreads, looking at the Bible on the small dresser. This was a mistake, Tom was thinking. They would be better off in Shaker Heights with all their things. Although— His mouth went dry. The thing they missed most was very near. He couldn't imagine life without him. His son. How proud he had been.

The doctor had come and gone, refusing any offers of Tom Jorrish to pay him.

Rachael stared at her hand. In the ball of a fist was a thirty-milligram dosage. "This will never put me to sleep, and you know it. Don't you have anything like a Valium?"

Tom shook his head sadly, needing sleep very badly. "Rachael, you've had about four Valiums. Do you think that's a good idea, sweetheart?"

"You know the only thing that puts me to sleep." Her eyes were glittering over the mascara bags underneath.

"I was thinking the same thing. I need you."

"And I need you," she agreed.

They made love and then slept until nine. When Tom awoke he could see Rachael sobbing and reaching into his jacket for the Valium. Mr. Chips. Only a night ago and yet he knew it would somehow put a wedge through their relationship.

* * *

THE Painseville jail. It didn't look like a penitentiary or prison or anything like that.

They put her in a room with another woman, who sat on the top bunk with her feet crossed. B.J. noticed she didn't wear matching socks.

"So you're here," the nameless woman said. "You'll miss breakfast but lunch is at noon. Maybe they'll let you get that. You're a real celebrity for killing that kid. You're a crazy girl."

"I didn't do it," B.J. protested, but she had a sore throat and it was hard to talk.

One of the matrons stood before them. She was striped. Everything was striped. The bars. She started to unlock the bars but thought better of it. "Hate to lose you, kid. One of your kin to see you."

B.J. retreated and watched as her brother was marched to the cell door. Shaking his head, he said, "I was sure you'd get yourself knocked up first. People are talking B.J., from the Bluebird Inn, to the general store, to every corner and even to North Madison. A reporter took my picture. They's swarming around like bumble bees in heat."

"Wilton, I did not kill that baby," B.J. said flatly.

"Well, I know that B.J. but you can't stop people from talking."

That was the nicest thing he had ever said to her. "But I'm here to tell you, you'll get no help from us. Grandmother, well, she thinks you did it. And Grandfather always follows. Doubt if Edward Bailey will marry you now."

Tears were streaming down her face. She wanted her friends. They would help her.

*Can't do anything to help you.* But wasn't that what families were for?

When he left, she finally slept for a few hours. She almost didn't wake up for lunch. When she did she thought only one thing: Wilton believed she didn't do it.

IT had been nearly dawn when he crept back to the house. Rich people. How he hated their ease and privilege. It had been easy to kill their baby; but then, it was easy to kill any baby. Like killing a fly. He had returned after a few days to check underneath the house for any traces of the marks made by the ladder. But not to worry. Just as he knew, though he had to double-check, there weren't any. The rain, that lucky-for-him rain, had washed everything away. The thin plastic rubber gloves he had used to hide all the fingerprints had been shredded so they looked like flies floating in the slimy water.

No, only one person had seen him. Oh, yes, talk about the perfect murder. This was it. Too perfect to be true.

# Chapter Six

"RUN that by me again," her cell mate, Pauli, said. She was trying to swat a fly with a flick of her wrist.

"It's *change of venue*," B.J. said. They had taken her into this room with all those people and they had said there was all this publicity as if it had been her fault.

Pauli was facedown on her stomach.

"That's for sure, sugar. Remember the reporter with a concealed camera who disguised himself as a visitor?"

B.J. looked around the jail. Not one of the kids had come to visit her. Nobody sent any cards or, at least, she didn't get them. Nobody cared except her newfound friend and cell mate, Pauli, wanted for larceny and fraud, awaiting her trial at the Painseville courthouse, knowing she would lose the battle.

"You know, doll face, I didn't like you much when you sashayed into my cell. But now I do like you and I want to tell you that you have been framed. You're takin' this rap for somebody and I just don't think you're capable of what they're saying you did."

"I've never even been to Cleveland," B.J. sobbed. "I've never been out of Madison except to Painseville and I didn't see much of it." Her hand clapped over her mouth. "Well, you know that I mean." For a second, she longed to tell her her secret dream, goal, wish for when they found the killer and let her go. Her grandparents would probably want her to leave. It might be easier to get up the hill and flag the bus. That's all she had to do.

"They'll acquit you, baby. Open-and-shut case. How could you have killed a baby?"

B.J. cried softly so Pauli could sleep. She was the only one who believed her innocent. The woman on the top bunk let her cry it out though it was painful for her to hear.

Then she thought for a moment and said, almost as an afterthought, "Listen, Kid. If it don't work out for you, I mean just the way you're telling it. I mean, if you find yourself doing time, just a word to the wise. Watch out for the other girls."

CLEVELAND, *Ohio, July 29, 1978.* The record-breaking heat showed no signs of letting up. Downtown Cleveland's department stores were almost empty. Halle's and Higbee's and even the May Company reported a loss in sales during the heat wave. As the temperature soared past ninety-five, Clevelanders stayed indoors with their air conditioners and fans, straying into the baby pool in their backyards. But they kept their televisions on.

Floor 16 of the building of the Cleveland Clerk had stuffed as many people as possible in the courthouse. With so many people sitting on the orange chairs crammed into the relatively small courtroom, it seemed like there was no air-conditioning at all. The onlookers and reporters were lined up and waiting in the hallway. As Clevelanders would have said, you could fry an egg on the streetwalk. Those that couldn't get in, jammed the downstairs for this trial of the beautiful teenage baby-sitter. Did she kill that baby? Yes or no?

The problem with the building was when it rained.

Because of some defect in the structure, it rained right into the building. But the people who crammed the downstairs weren't that lucky. There was so much humidity already, they were wet enough. Upstairs where five chairs had been left for the public, they stared at the Great Seal of Ohio and thought nothing like this had happened since they had tried the now long-dead Sam Sheppard in 1955.

This was the first day of the trial. The jury selection had been finalized the day before in the pretrial, and bail had been set at $150,000, so high that the courtroom got out of control and the judge had to bang his gavel for order. B.J. had sat staring, knowing that even if the bail were $50, her grandparents would have left her to rot in jail, anyway.

Dizzy from the oppressive heat, she walked through the circus of reporters and television cameras, her eyes on the ground. She was told to say nothing and was led in arm in arm, by her lawyer from Legal Aid, a young man who had himself been arrested for protesting the Vietnam War, a nobody who had suddenly been propelled into the national spotlight.

Mort Shwartz had brought her the pale blue waist-shirt, but no shoes, so she wore her sneakers without socks. He told her to tie her hair back into a ponytail and not to wear any makeup, but he didn't tell her why.

Inside the courtroom, jam-packed with people, the air-conditioning was almost as low as the humidity was high. She heard a shrill scream and saw someone was parting shoulders, rushing toward her. Suddenly she was being held so tightly she thought she had stopped breathing.

Hands parted them as the person said, "B.J., it's me!"

"Debbie? Debbiiee!" B.J. yelled and jumped up and down in the heat as if they had been talking about a boyfriend.

She smiled and kissed her best friend and Mort liked the way that looked, so he didn't interfere.

"I'm sorry I couldn't visit you in Painseville . . . but my mom wouldn't let me."

B.J. suddenly realized there were thousands of eyes looking at her. Debbie's mother wouldn't let her come to jail. B.J. had felt nothing before, but now she felt angry and envious. Debbie was baby-sitting and going to the carnivals in the Township Park and swimming in the lake and sneaking a beer with all the kids at the Bluebird. All B.J. had seen was the inside of a dirty, smelly jail.

"Not too long, B.J.," Mort whispered, tapping her on the shoulder. She looked up into his friendly brown eyes and thought he would be her mother now.

"All the kids are here," Debbie was saying. B.J. looked around for their eyes. "We wanted to have a bake sale to raise money for your bail but . . ."

B.J. nodded. Too many cakes. They could never do it. But they had tried. They cared. Mort was trying to hurry her along now to take their seats at the defense table.

Debbie followed after her. "But this is the important news, Beej. Listen, that night when Hughie wanted to see you, he did come by and it was him who rang the doorbell and . . ."

B.J. turned, her eyes bright. "Hughie thinks he saw someone get away. He thinks he saw the killer."

B.J. watched Debbie disappear into the crowd. Then she saw that Mort was telling her to sit down. He pointed to the jurors. There were twelve people and four alternate members of the jury.

She nodded and, in a second, she was all smiles. Hughie had seen the killer and he would testify that she was telling the truth. She closed her eyes and thought, fervently, of the dream, the long road, the suitcase, flagging down the bus. Smiling, she knew she would make it. She was going to be free!

More than a few of the sedate jurors looked over and saw the bubbly, radiant teenager almost unable to contain herself. Alarmed, Mort passed her a note: *What's up?*

B.J. laughed and turned it over, writing, *"Good news. Hughie saw the killer that night."* Mort started to come around behind her and talk to her, at least tell her to get that shit-kicking grin off of her pretty face but the trial was beginning. It took a long time to ask for quiet. The deputy sheriff was setting out the pitchers of water and hooking up the microphones for the lawyers, the judge, and the witness stand.

He looked around. All over the room people were waving makeshift fans out of hats and newspapers. Some in the back coughed. A whole row of people coughed and then it seemed as if the whole courtroom was coughing and then it stopped abruptly. The judge, now seated, looked out from a high bench around the room.

B.J. looked into the judge's eyes and felt immediately afraid. He reminded her of Grandmother. The judge banged his gavel. Soon he would see that it was a mistake, a mistrial. Everybody could go home.

She watched as the prosecuting attorney rose to begin his opening statement. What struck her from the first was how different he looked from the lawyer they had given her. He was wearing a pin-striped suit with a black-and-white tie and a red handkerchief. As if he was unaffected by the heat. He looked like a paper doll. Mort looked like he could use a shower.

She watched his mouth move and knew he liked his words. She tuned out and made up stories about the people in the courtroom that she could finish later when they took her back to jail. But she awoke with an abrupt start when she heard him lying.

". . . and ladies and gentlemen of the jury, Betty Jo Stronger is charged with murder in the second degree."

She closed her eyes, hugging herself with her arms, rocking backwards and smiling slyly. He was wrong. Eat your words, prosecuting attorney, she wanted to yell as tears rolled down her face. Why was she here? She had prayed to God for help.

Like in a play, he went on and on and she tried, like in a play, to be in the audience. But it was hard. So hard.

"It was a normal Saturday night when the baby-sitter, Miss Betty Jo Stronger, was driven into Madison by Thomas Jorrish. It was raining that night, a hard, thrashing rain. Rachael Jorrish gave her baby-sitter a selection of fine clothes and even had a dinner in the oven. The only thing wrong about that Saturday night seemed to be the stormy weather.

"But a little after eleven that night the Jorrishes returned. Unbeknownst to them, their little baby, Joshua, thirteen months old, in the prime of health, lay dead in his crib upstairs. Now ladies and gentlemen of the jury—what happened in between those hours when the baby was alive and the baby was dead? I'll tell you what happened . . ."

He couldn't tell them what had happened. He didn't actually know what had happened. *Ladies and gentlemen of the jury, he's making it up,* she wanted to shout. Instead, she sat with her legs spread apart. She didn't notice Mort trying to tell her to sit up straight. No one had given her any deodorant in that jail and now there would be big circles under her arms because she was sweating. She noticed Wilton, sitting in the front row. He had gotten a new kind of haircut, not so much of a crew cut. It looked like an army haircut. She chuckled to herself. Anything to stop that noise of the mean man's mouth and the lies he was telling. In the fourth row beyond Wilton, she noticed her drama teacher, Mrs.

Bernett. She had come. Scanning quickly around, she spotted the kids. They were all scattered around. The courtroom was filled with her friends.

The prosecuting attorney was finished his speech now.

"And so for a brief, fleeting moment that Saturday night, May the fifth, the Jorrishes were a happy family. But now they have buried their little baby and with him their happy life."

At first it sounded like a sneeze but, with anxiety, Mort recognized it as an anguished sob and it was coming from one of the women in the jury. He looked over at B.J., who was smiling confidently about God knows what, and then he watched that sunny mood give way to a storm of sudden tears. Hurriedly he passed back his crumpled handkerchief to her, wondering what was going on. This wasn't the image they had rehearsed, not the sweet teenager on trial for her life.

B.J. started to hiccup then and couldn't stop. Mort reached around and poured her a glass of water and as he did the lining in his newly mended jacket began to rip and he had to remove it for the rest of the trial. It was the only suit he had. There was a hush all around them. You could almost hear the quiet as Rachael Jorrish was escorted to the witness stand and sworn in by the bailiff. B.J. memorized how smart she looked so she could think about it later in her cell. She wore a royal-blue silk suit and a tailored white blouse and blue pumps. And she was stuffed with Valium and had had a short vial of vodka. B.J. leaned in to hang on every word that she would say, knowing she didn't really want to hear it.

There was no one in the stuffy courtroom who did not have his or her eyes on the beautiful Rachael Jorrish, who looked a lot like Princess Di. With one shapely leg crossed over another, she looked strangely alert. That's why B.J. couldn't figure it out later. There was a loud hum in the small, but packed room. Everyone waited. She opened her mouth to speak and slumped in her chair. A loud hum, almost a contagious buzz filled the room and some people got up to try and help her. Rachael Jorrish had passed out. Tom Jorrish rushed up to his wife and waved away the cup of water offered. While everyone watched, he lifted her in his arms and carried her out just as she came to and wailed, "My baby, my baby, bring back my baby."

Several people wept with her, including two of the women on the jury. Mort covered his face in his hands. Things couldn't be worse.

The judge called a twenty-minute break after that. A newspaper someone had been fanning themselves with landed on a chair close to B.J. She picked up *The Cleveland Plain Dealer* and saw her picture was smack on the cover. The same dreamy, faraway picture that made her look not much older than a girl scout. Why had they given out that picture? She looked like she was focusing on some mysterious dot in the sky or awaiting further instructions. Mort was tugging at her sleeve and the thousand eyes were watching her but she couldn't stop reading.

"Rachael Jorrish, mother of the deceased baby, claimed that she believed B.J. Stronger of Madison-on-the-Lake, Ohio, was psychiatrically disturbed before the time of the murder, but hid it from the Shaker Heights couple. Rachael Jorrish, 36, said today that B.J. Stronger killed the baby to perform some kind of sick ritual to erase her envy of the Jorrishes."

B.J. stared straight ahead while people milled about all around her. Like the people in the courtroom, she almost believed she killed that baby. She could see herself strapped to an electric chair.

"It's a lie," B.J. screamed.

Most of the courtroom had kept their seats, because it was just too hot to move. The judge had disappeared

69

into his chambers. Mort tried to quiet her. All of the front sections could hear her scream. Those in the back strained forward. Many knew it was a "scene" before she screamed again. "Rachael Jorrish is a liar! Did you see that paper!" It just went on for a few seconds but people were looking and Mort, helpless, clamped his hand over her mouth. At the same time, she jerked her head around and the rubber band holding the carefully crafted ponytail snapped, leaving her hair to fall in her face.

"Now, listen," he said, stooping down by her chair. "B.J., I know this is hard for you. That you're just a kid. But you're on trial for your life. People will say things to make you angry."

B.J. was silent now, suddenly ashamed of her screaming fit. It was just that everyone who read that paper would believe Rachael Jorrish was telling the truth. And she wasn't. She was lying.

Mort reached in his pocket and pulled out a small plastic vial. "I want you to take these. These will calm you down, B.J."

She looked at the tiny pills in her hand. He handed her a cup of water and she swallowed the tranquillizers obediently, gulping and crying at the same time.

TOWARD the end of the sticky day, they had seen a parade of witnesses called to the stand. Elmo, dear Elmo, who pulled at his necktie. His men had measured the window. It was clear that someone could have placed a ladder at the bottom and climbed up and in. And her drama teacher, such a sweet, little old lady, said such nice things about her. Even Mort was relaxed for the first time.

She was called up to the witness stand and yawned. Slowly she took her seat, feeling very good indeed, almost mellowed. She scanned the table of exhibits, the knife, the baby's pillow, even his little yellow jammies.

Mort was talking to her. "You saw the window closed and then you rushed back up the steps because you remembered you had opened it? Is that correct?"

B.J. worked her mouth, stifling a yawn so she looked ladylike to please Mort. It was so hot in the courtroom, like a too warm bathtub. She looked around at the eyes and saw that they had mouths under them. If she stood on her head, all the mouths would be upside down.

Her eyelids felt heavy and her tongue was thick. Good Lord, what had she swallowed so obediently? Her head became heavy and fell down to her chest but she jerked it back up. Someone was talking to her.

Mort, pacing up and down as the prosecuting attorney had, looked out at his audience and asked B.J., "When did you first notice the baby was dead?"

There was no answer.

"I said, when did you first notice the baby was dead?"

He turned to his client. There were titterings and outright laughter. As he turned, to his horror he saw that B.J. in her carefully selected cornflower blue dress, with her knees spread out, her head on her shoulder, had fallen asleep.

# Chapter Seven

THERE was a ripple of laughter in the courtroom and Mort felt his neck redden. Quickly he shook her awake whispering, "B.J., please don't do this."

Immediately she was awake, wondering why the judge was laughing at her. Then it was quiet except for the faint swishing of fans as people strained to hear her speak. But there was something wrong with the way she spoke and as he listened to her voice, he felt a sinking feeling in his gut. This was worse than ever. He would never give her a tranquillizer again.

He wanted to beg her to weep, stumble, wrench the jurors' hearts, be a teenager. Instead, she was doing this phony precise imitation of some British actress. Where did she get that from? She was so distant. So without emotion. So cold-blooded. What was she trying to do? Send herself to the gas chamber?

Reluctantly, he looked from the corner of his eye at the jurors. He felt the nauseating chill of pure panic rise in him as he tried to go on. The jurors were expressionless, as if they had judged her already. Mort Shwartz could see then that he had made a bad mistake. He hadn't plea-bargained this case. He had been so sure they would find this sweet, natural teenager not guilty, not capable of committing such a horrible crime. Things seemed to be slipping away like sand seeping through his fingers. Nothing was going the way he had planned it. There was no evidence.

Sometimes he woke up in the middle of the night fighting the damp sheets, sweating like a pig, and it was always the same horrible nightmare. He saw his client strangling that baby with her own two hands. And then he saw her lean back her head, laughing. A strange haunting for a lawyer who believed his client was innocent.

As he looked at her, he thought it didn't do her any good that she was so gorgeous. That's why he had ordered the little ponytail and the fresh-scrubbed look. He knew what she looked like—every man's lustful fantasy of the ripe-as-peaches look. The sexy baby-sitter, so close, so willing. Just as he knew that women in the room hated her for her movie-star looks.

The next witness after B.J.'s disaster was her grandmother, Mrs. Stronger. Everyone waited sympathetically, including the bailiff who would swear her in, while she lumbered slowly to the chair. She sat down in a floral dress that resembled a house dress and spread her legs open, revealing knee-high stockings. One thing Mary Stronger was sure of, she didn't like the young man next to her. He wasn't a Christian, God help him. She didn't like pushy fellows with the gift of gab. One of them had sold her a radio that wouldn't work. Besides that man, she had never talked to a Jew in her whole life and she had no intention of satisfying him now. He needed a new haircut, that's what was missing. Liberals were all alike.

"Mrs. Stronger. How long have you been your granddaughter's legal guardian?" he had the nerve to ask her.

"Let's see. That's almost fifteen years. She was a handful then and she's a handful now."

There was a roll of laughter like a wave when the

tide breaks. The old woman smiled, liking the feeling that she had the power to make all those fools laugh. The judge banged his gavel. B.J. wasn't laughing. She used to call them "Grandma" and "Grandpa" but she quickly learned what they wanted. To somehow grow up feeling guilty for a crime she knew nothing about. Now they had their crime and they were playing it to the hilt. When she was little, she had asked herself over and over, Whatever did I do wrong? When she had been very little she thought it was because she didn't have that thing between her legs. No, it wasn't that. It was something else.

"Were you surprised to learn of the death of the Jorrish baby the night B.J. had her baby-sitting job?"

The old lady smirked and it was unmistakable on her graying face. Nice way of phrasing things, he had.

"No," she said simply.

There was a murmuring throughout the small courtroom and the judge banged his gavel for attention with the usual threats he hadn't done anything about. Mort pulled at his collar and knew he was sweating. God, couldn't they turn the air conditioner on higher?

"Surely, you're not saying that you expected your granddaughter, a mere teenager, to kill that helpless baby, are you?"

"I wouldn't put anything past her," said the old lady flatly.

Again the judge had to bang his gavel.

Mort rocked back on his heels. He was sure the temperature had risen to 105 in the last hour. He looked over at his client, sitting cool as a cucumber, staring at her grandmother. He wanted to shake her shoulders until her head wobbled and say, "Please, cry, do something, don't just sit there like a store mannequin."

Didn't she know when people weren't watching the drama on stage they were stealing looks at her to judge her reactions? He should tell her. He should have told her a lot of things. Finally, finally, the nasty, possibly senile woman climbed off the chair. Mort couldn't breathe. He felt like the heat would suffocate him. He only knew he had thrown a bone in the prosecuting attorney's way.

It was after lunch when the prosecuting attorney called Debbie Newsom to the stand. B.J. saw again that she had cut her hair into soft curls. She liked it but there was no way she could tell her.

Debbie was wearing a pink full skirt and pink heels and a white blouse. Her churchgoing clothes, B.J. thought. Now they would interview the kids and it would all go better for her. Her friends knew she couldn't kill Josh. She had wanted to cry when her grandmother had said all those ugly things about her. But she had learned over the years never to cry at anything she said. She would not give the old woman that satisfaction. Sometimes she wondered, Where did the tears go? She had stopped letting her grandparents bother her.

But right now she felt bothered. What could she do? The usual. Stuff it. Keep a stiff upper lip.

She watched the other attorney. He looked like he just stepped out of a men's fashion magazine. She glanced over at her lawyer and then quickly away. Mort resembled an unmade bed.

Mort, sitting beside her now, leaned over and nudged her to pay attention. He didn't have to do that. This was Debbie. And she knew how uncomfortable Debbie got having to speak to a lot of people.

She nodded but didn't turn.

"Was the defendant your best friend?"

B.J. held her breath. She had thought they were.

"Yes, sir, B.J. was my best friend."

B.J. smiled. She had thought so.

"So I imagine you exchanged secrets then, didn't you, Ms. Newsom?"

B.J. bit her lip. Not every secret.

"We talked on the phone almost every night when she could."

"Were you, in fact, talking on the phone the night of the murder?"

B.J. got a funny, quirky feeling in the bottom of her stomach, which had nothing in it but that wilty salad Mort had bought for her.

"Yes," Debbie said.

"Did B.J. say anything about the baby-sitting job or the baby?"

There were tears flowing down Debbie's cheeks. "That's hard to say. It was raining very hard and—"

"Did she say anything about the baby?"

Debbie swung her left foot and started to bite her nails.

"She didn't talk about her baby-sitting job at all?"

Silence.

"Remember, Deborah, you're under oath. You just swore on a Bible."

Debbie studied her pink heels she had picked up for half-price. Her voice trembling, she said, "Well, sir, the baby was crying a lot and she said something about that . . ."

Just a tinge of impatience in his voice but it was also kind. Debbie felt confused. She fingered the silver cross she always wore, not even taking it off to take a shower. When she spoke, her voice was almost inaudible and her face was almost as pink as her skirt. Shutting her eyes, still fondling her cross, Debbie recited, "She said, 'Honest, I could kill that baby,' sir, but I think it was some kind of joke." There was an immediate murmur in the first row of chairs.

Mort immediately jumped to his feet. "Objection, your honor."

"Objection sustained, but only if the defense attorney can hold back some of his enthusiasm. This is not a civil rights trial." Mort sat down, knowing that no one had heard the last part of what she had said. There was a thunderous noise in the courtroom. Mort reached for a glass of water and then, gulping down too much, choked and started coughing for air and someone had to slap him on the back.

B.J. shut her eyes as if to seal in the pain. Debbie would go to church tonight to pray for her soul and confess that she had to say what she said because it was right.

But it was wrong, too.

Why did the judge with the white hair whom she liked to pretend was the Pope, why did he have to bang his gavel like that? Why didn't he just shout "Quiet, quiet in the courtroom" through a microphone?

She watched as her tall, lanky brother strode up, took the oath, and looked over the eager faces as if he wanted to sell them something. Wilton liked an audience. It warmed him almost as much as a nice ale. B.J. took a clump of her hair and twirled it around her finger and her forefinger, and Mort wasn't there to pull her hand away.

Mort was staring at the brother B.J. had warned him about. It looked like he had cut his hair with a lawn mower or just got out of basic training. Cocky son of a bitch. Why couldn't she have a nice, normal family that sat on the witness stand and sobbed out her innocence?

He took a deep breath. Here went nothing. Tonight he would go home and have an ice-cold shower and then a chilled screwdriver with three ice cubes—and cigarettes, lots of cigarettes. After he had reviewed the case, Mort began his interrogation of her brother, whatever his name was, and he immediately thought of some chopped round steak he had put in the freezer and that had gone bad.

"Did your sister baby-sit for anyone else other than the Jorrishes?" Dumb question. Anyone who called. And then she forked over half of her earnings to the house.

"Yessir. But the Jorrishes was her favorite."

*Was?* Did he graduate Madison High or what? Dig deeper, question. "Do you think your sister, B.J., was in any way envious of the Jorrishes or their life-style?"

Pause. "No, sir. No, I don't think of B.J. as the envious type."

Mort tried not to appear caught off guard. Where would be the surprise attack? He switched gears.

"When your parents were killed in the automobile accident you came to live with . . . your grandparents. So you are originally from Cleveland? Is that correct?"

"Yessir."

Shit. The seam ripped again. He would be lucky if he wasn't standing there naked at the end of the day. Something was bothering Mort and he didn't know what. Maybe it was just that he was a simple legal-aide lawyer and now he had this. He hadn't wanted it.

"How did you feel toward your sister when you were growing up? What was she like?"

"Well, we fought some. All siblings do that, don't they? Protective, that's what I felt."

B.J. shook her head. That's not how it was at all.

"Do you think your sister could have killed the Jorrish baby?"

There was a deafening silence. Finally Wilton spoke. He had an engaging grin and a few people up close smiled with him. "No, sir, I guess I don't. B.J. was terrified of death. She was just a little kid when her parents died that night on the highway. She couldn't kill a bug. Not even if her head is messed up, which it usually is."

78

Mort looked over at B.J., who was staring straight ahead not blinking. Next came the kid they were waiting for. The rich kid who had been hot for her panties and came all the way in the rain to play with the babysitter.

Mort didn't like rich kids. He understood this one was going to go to law school. Wouldn't have any trouble getting in, either. He was sure, too, he wouldn't have to wait tables to do it.

As Hugh was being sworn in, B.J. thought how funny everyone looked without their bathing suits. Hughie was wearing a suit and tie. He looked so different. She held her breath. Dear Hughie, he had loved her. All the kids had loved her and in a not-very-long time, she would be free because Hughie had seen the killer run away.

Mort revved himself into courtroom technique that he personally abhorred. He would warm into this boy's testimony, build it, and then deliver the crescendo.

"What college will you be going to in the fall?"

"Harvard."

"Did you ask B.J. for a date the night of the murder?"

"That afternoon. But she had said she had to babysit and she couldn't have any visitors."

Mort smiled understandably. "But you went over anyway."

He looked over at his well-dressed parents.

"No, sir, I didn't. Why would I? If she said no."

Mort stumbled for a second, trying not to show how panicked he was. Modulating his voice, he said, "I'm sorry. Did I hear you say that . . ."

"No, sir, it wasn't me," said the snobby, sleazy, goddammned son of a bitch. "I was at home with my parents."

"I have to remind you that you're under oath and—"

"Objection," the prosecuting attorney said.

"Objection overruled, continue, Mr. Shwartz."

Mort cleared his throat. If he hadn't gone to the house, he hadn't rung the doorbell, and that meant he hadn't seen the killer run away from the house. He wished he could take out his handkerchief and mop his brow—wasn't that the expression? But now he was beginning to think his biggest mistake was in having that salami sandwich and beer for lunch. If he hadn't gone to the house, rung the doorbell, and seen the killer, then somebody was lying.

"So you weren't at the Jorrish house the night of the murder?"

"I told you I wasn't," Hughie snapped somewhat arrogantly. Mort nodded. There were no witnesses. He had an alibi. B.J. sat with her mouth opened, shaking her head. He was wrong. Wrong. Debbie had said he had seen the killer.

Somebody was lying and Mort had a hunch it was that bratty little rich kid, Hugh.

A few days after the heat wave broke, the jury was taken to a Holiday Inn. They deliberated for seven days, sending notes out to the judge. B.J. sat in one position in her cell, unable to eat, unable to sleep, unable to think for herself at all. She couldn't even figure out how to tie the shoelaces on her sneakers.

Only Mort came to see her in those final days. He assured her of an acquittal, and so of course he had to be right. Just a matter of days and she would be back in Madison with the kids. Maybe she could stay at Debbie's house before she left for New York. He became her constant companion; together they waited, together they prayed.

One thing Mort was sure of. He could read a jury. They weren't about to convict a seventeen-year-old girl. Not this jury.

On the eighth day, B.J. was taken back to the court-house on the arm of her lawyer. She sat down, hands folded, ramrod straight, waiting for the jury. Mort had told her the verdict would be "not guilty" but she had to hear those words. Until she heard them, her life was hanging in the balance.

Minutes stretched unbearably and she wanted to push the hands of the clock forward. The judge was staring at her and he was talking. But midway through her hands flew over her ears as she heard the ugly word over and over. She shook her head violently, no, no, no. Mort had to be held up as he almost passed out.

"Guilty . . . guilty . . . guilty . . ." The judge banged his gavel but no one heard it over the uproar in the courtroom.

No one rushed to help her. She felt strange, as if she'd been beaten up. Everybody hated her. She could feel the ugly stares. Looking around, she shrank phys-ically into herself. She retreated to that funny dot in her mind where she could escape and think about noth-ing for hours.

"Guilty on all counts," the judge said when the din had quieted down. "I sentence you to ten years to life, with no parole until after ten years and it is also deemed that the first year of your sentence should be spent in the Columbus State Hospital for the Insane."

The gavel banged again. People stood up talking. It reminded B.J. of church. Watching detached, she saw the big silver handcuffs and the hands being whipped behind her, she looked into the whirling television cam-eras and saw the already familiar-looking reporters. This time Mort was nowhere to be seen as she was led out by a matron. "Keep it moving," someone said. The reporters were walking with them.

"Do you intend to appeal the case?" a reporter asked her and Mort spoke up. "Yes, of course we'll appeal."

Then B.J. came out of that private place in her mind

and began to screech, "No, it's a lie! I'm innocent. Please believe me. Oh God, believe me. I didn't kill that baby!"

She held on to Mort as long as she could, embracing him, until the matron pried her away. Then a car door opened and she sat in the car of the deputy sheriff, who would drive her back to the Painseville jail for the last time.

# BOOK

# II

# Chapter Eight

AN agonizing, haunting scream filled the hallway. Then there was silence, an ugly silence.

B.J. shivered. Someone was in trouble. Shouldn't they check? But no one did.

A woman ran up to her, pulling at her skirt, pleading, "Got a cigarette, got a cigarette . . ."

Her hand was out like a street beggar and B.J. brushed it away stuttering, "I don't smoke."

"Move it along," the woman in front of her demanded.

The walls were drab olive green with dirt marks all over them. On a bulletin board were cutouts of fall leaves that said DOCTOR, NURSE, SOCIAL WORKER, RECREATIONAL THERAPIST. The patients had done this themselves in the Occupational Therapy room. Some of the leaves were falling off.

B.J. followed the woman into a room with four beds and green steel lockers.

The woman had whitish-gray hair pulled back into a knot on top of her head. Nurses' aide was the only job she could get. It gave her a chance to vent her little angers on these druggy, dopey patients who had no control over their lives. This was the part of the job she looked forward to.

"Take off your clothes," she ordered.

B.J. stared, rubbing the sore spot where the handcuffs had cut too deeply.

"Strip!" she yelled. "Everything. Panties. Bra."

It was the middle of the day but B.J. did as she was told, feeling her face get hot as the woman studied her. She was given a set of freshly laundered pajamas. She liked the way they smelled but the tops were dark blue and the bottoms were dishwater gray. Struggling to get into them, she saw the sleeves came below her hands and the pants were slipping below her waist.

"Too big," B.J. said.

The woman's eyes were slanted as if her bun had been pulled too tight. B.J. wondered if that was why she was so surly. Little hairs stood out above her upper lip and she sneered at the beautiful girl before her.

"Listen, missy," she said in a low, rumbling voice, because they all had weak spots. They could all be controlled. "I don't take kindly to young girls who take a notion to murder helpless babies just for the thrill of it, you hear?"

B.J. started to protest but the Charlie Chaplin pants had slipped down.

"I followed your whole trial. Don't think you're some sort of a star here. We have rules and regulations in this place. Follow the rules and you won't get hurt."

B.J. stared at the floor, afraid to look up. *Hurt?* Didn't she mean she wouldn't get into trouble?

There was a slam and a click and she realized her clothes had been locked away. She was handed a long piece of gauze to tie her bottoms at the waist. There was nowhere else to go except out into the hall, but B.J. felt afraid to move from the room. She felt safe there.

It will be okay, she told herself. Mort was going for an appeal. They would let her out soon. There had been mistakes in the trial. She wouldn't have to be here long.

She eyed the long hall outside the door. People were just drifting up and down, passing by, talking to no one. And she noticed the same glassy stare in their eyes as they walked nowhere.

She wanted to run, but there was no where to go.

"How you doin', honey bun?"

B.J. turned around to the kind voice and saw a roly-poly black girl with two front teeth missing and cheeks like apples.

B.J. opened her mouth to speak but the girl started singing so loud she would have to scream to be heard. She walked into the large room at the end of the hall. In one corner there was a black-and-white television that skipped up and down. Off to the side was a sagging Ping-Pong table but she couldn't see any paddles or balls. In the bookshelf, she thumbed through dusty books that had been written in the thirties and forties. In the far end of the room was a woman who sat knees up to her face, rocking and singing low. In a high-backed wooden chair there was a man who kept un-snapping his pajamas, pulling out his penis, and then stuffing it back.

But it was the stale smell of urine that she found the hardest to take.

My God, she asked no one, how could people live like this?

One by one they came up.

"Hi, when are you getting out?"

"Hi, what are you on?"

"Cigarette? Do you have just one, I'll pay you back, tomorrow my sister's coming and . . ."

B.J. put her hands over her ears to shut them up. She didn't want to make friends. She couldn't spend an-other minute in this place. It wasn't fair. She didn't belong here. All the pent-up rage came bubbling out through her mouth. "No, no, I can't bear it. Not one more minute." Some of the patients backed away from her, thinking she was building up to an anger she couldn't control. Maybe she'd have convulsions. But they stayed in the room because they lived for this kind of scenario.

B.J. kept screaming, not caring. People were running down the hall. A fat aide grabbed her by her arms. A male nurse threw her on the floor and lowered her pajamas. She felt the sharp prick of a needle but she couldn't stop screaming.

She was dragged, by her armpits, down the hall. A door was opened and she was literally tossed into the room like a caged wild animal. Snapping her head around, she heard the door lock. It was dark and on the floor was a thin mattress covered with a sheet. Catching her breath, not sure what had come over her, she noticed something smelled. It was the mattress. It was covered with brown stuff. She backed away. It was covered with shit.

The window looking into the room was small, big enough for a face. One by one, the patients framed themselves in the square porthole. They made faces, sticking out their tongues, stretching their mouths long and wide. "No, no," she whispered.

Then she banged on the door until her hands hurt, yelling, "Let me out. Let me out!" But no one came.

MEDS. After that they gave her small brown pills to take and they looked like M&M's, but if you crunched into them, it was a little like biting into iron. Her hands had started to curl. She began to see double, her mouth felt like sandpaper and she was thirsty. Oh, Coke. She would have given anything for a Coca-Cola with ice so the bubbles went to the top.

But she never had any visitors.

Why would anyone want to come to the crazy house?

Sometimes she forgot how she got there. It seemed so long ago. That day she was slipping down the hall in her green Styrofoam slippers with the cutout smile face imprinted on them. She had gotten that free. Just like the blue toothbrush and the comb. But she wanted a Coca-Cola.

She wasn't listening when her name was called out. She wasn't used to hearing her name and also she wasn't sure that was her name. Sometimes.

"Stronger, what the hell's the matter with you, girl? You deaf and mute? I already know you'se are dumb."

She spun around. "I didn't do anything wrong."

"You got a visitor."

A visitor. There must be some mistake, she thought.

"B.J. Where can we go to talk?"

It was Mort. He was dressed in jeans and a plaid shirt and his hair was very stylishly done, the curls were gone.

He handed her a silver-topped box with a bright pink ribbon and she led him into the stinking dayroom. They sat opposite each other at a table with small chairs. She peeked inside the box and saw there were chocolates and then rocked and sang to herself. A little birdie had told him what she wanted. She craved chocolate. The meds did that. Almost as much as Coca-Cola.

"B.J.," Mort said, "are you okay?"

"Okay." She smiled, biting into half of each piece and then putting the other half gingerly aside.

"B.J., what's wrong? Did I offend you in anyway? Did I say something bad? Actually, I came here with good news." And he came here because of the gut-gnawing guilt that woke him up in the middle of the night. That he had failed her. That he had lost it somehow, sold out.

She was debating between something soft with a shiny red wrapping or a sugar-coated almond she could just crunch. Out of the corner of her eye, she noticed him and said, "Why did you come here? My life is over."

Mort felt the tears in his eyes. He started to say something he couldn't. This case had made him a national celebrity. He had a new job, a new apartment, a new car, and dates with women who never would have looked his way before. But he had lost the case. It didn't matter.

"I'm crazy, didn't you know that?" She licked her fingers hunting for another piece.

Suddenly Mort snatched the box away from her savagely. He leaned in. "Now, you listen to me. You pull yourself together, you hear? I'm going for an appeal and we have a good chance to win. I don't want to see you like this. You're not crazy, but this place will drive you crazy."

He studied the play of emotions in her face. Such a beautiful face but a dirty face, sticky hair, vacant eyes. He wanted her to be beautiful again. So he could sleep.

He left her sitting there looking at the ravaged box of chocolates. She smiled but he had already left. Then she looked around. Someone was staring at her. She had learned to feel it rather than see it. When she looked around, there was nothing. It had been that way for a while. There were the eyes. And then they disappeared.

JINGLE bells, jingle bells, jingle all the way. He popped the flip-top off a frosty can of beer and toasted the announcement on the television. Three days until Christmas and Santa had brought him a gift.

He looked outside where there was a lot of what looked like cotton candy. The Christmas tree had lights but no one had plugged it in.

So he was free for sure now. Unconditionally. The beer dribbled down his chin and he hiccuped.

She wasn't.

B.J. looked out at the snow for a long time. She couldn't go out and scoop some up, letting it fall through her fingers like sugar. The television played continuously on the weekends starting early at nine o'clock. They were awakened at 6:00 A.M. so they wouldn't be late.

She was trying to listen to it, but the latest really bad patient kept turning it off. There was nothing to do. Nothing to do. She could walk up and down the big hall but she had just done that. Ever since Mort had come she had shampooed her hair twice a week with the coarse blue liquid the State provided. Her face was washed every day and her nails were clean and short. Of all the losses she felt, it was her nails. They were long and they should be pretty. Even the nurses had noticed her and told her she was getting better but she didn't know what had been wrong with her.

Half looking at the television, half studying a new patient, her mouth fell open in horror. She was in shock. She thought Mort would have told her. He should have been the one.

The announcer had told her and she might as well have skipped out: "The state of Ohio and the Court of Appeals have denied appeal to Betty Jo Stronger, the convicted killer of baby Joshua Jorrish. The murder happened last May in the resort town of Madison-on-the-Lake."

No one had told her. And she had no one to tell. The tears that spilled out of her eyes landed on the plastic couch. One of the patients, in a striped bathrobe, came waltzing over and tipped her chin up. B.J. shuddered and pushed him away as he said, "Hey, whatsa matter? How about a game of Scrabble? You promised." She would never be free. That's what the news meant. She pushed him away and, angrily, he began to pull her hair.

"Stop it, leave me alone!" she said. But he kept putting his hands on her. She reached out, furious, and pulled the belt on his robe. Then she started to laugh.

She could tell and then *he'd* get the Quiet Room, not her.

She began to scream and cry and an aide came into the room, "Ladies and gentlemen, you are doubling our load of paperwork." To the short man/boy she said, "You'll have to get rid of your belt. I'll snip it off when I do the meds. Remind me."

Then she turned on B.J. "One more scene like that and I'll put you in the Quiet Room. I for one can't figure you out. One day you're the model patient. Another you're sick."

"Well . . . uh . . . I . . ."

"He started it," another patient mumbled, then thought better of it. A group had formed, eager to break up the relentless boredom with a scene.

Gasping for breath, her chest heaving, hair wildly in her eyes, B.J. snapped her head around. "What?" she said but there was no one behind her. The eyes, she had felt the eyes again. Always staring. Always waiting. And then they would disappear to leave her wondering if they had been there at all.

But they had. Someone was watching her. Waiting.

She looked around the dayroom. The patients had lost interest by now. The nurses had returned to their station down the hall. *Have denied appeal, convicted killer of baby* thundered in her mind and she clamped hands over ears to stamp it out.

She watched the big clock move another minute. On the floor cockroaches were working their way toward four broken crayons. Someone had torn the pages out of a book and stacked them neatly on the bookshelf. There was gaspy, jagged breathing and she realized, surprised, that she was the one making that noise.

So that was it. He had lied to her. Again. She wasn't going to be free. Ever. There was no way out of anything, really. Tears trickled down her cheeks as she picked up the broken crayons.

She was seventeen and she had no future. Nothing to live for.

Nobody gave a damn.

God helps those who help themselves, Grandmother had told her.

There was a way to help herself.

Escape.

# Chapter Nine

THEY threw a little party for her, the night before she was eighteen. Eighteen was a milestone age. Girls went to proms, had boyfriends, went off to college. She sat next to Evelyn, who had a frontal lobotomy when she was eighteen. Now she was ageless, and sat flicking her thumb and forefinger back and forth on her nose. That was the only thing she did.

Sarah had brought a bag of potato chips. Milty had brought a half-gone bag of hard candies. There were no drinks, no sodas, no juices. But there was a stack of paper cups for water. Paper cups were usually hard to come by.

"Happy Birthday to you.

"Happy Birthday to you . . ."

Their voices soared and crackled and a few forgot the words. A young black boy in the next chair leaned over and fell asleep on her shoulder.

A whole year had gone by. She would be eighteen tomorrow and now she could go off to prison. Lifting an empty paper cup, she toasted herself. She remembered when she had tried to escape. Each time she tried to get out the door, she had been caught. And each time they had put her in the Quiet Room. But B.J. knew they couldn't do anything to her or for her. She was just being baby-sitted until she was ready for prison. There was no way to escape. You could only escape somewhere in your mind.

It was hot for late fall and in the hospital the air had been there for a long time. She began to fan herself with her hand. She was remembering the stifling heat and stickiness of her trial. In one whole year she hadn't heard from anyone. Not one of the kids had ever sent her a card. They had stayed away on purpose. They believed the lies that she had done it. She hadn't. Or were they right and she had? It was hard to replay, to see where innocence was and what people had said about her, to her face, telling her that she was wrong.

"Clean up!" someone yelled and that was the end of her impromptu birthday party. The greasy potato chip bag was crunched, invisible crumbs were meticulously scraped off the table, and the little cups were marched dutifully to the nurses' aide. B.J. looked around sharply. Someone was watching her. But when she turned around no one was there.

"Happy Birthday, B.J.," she whispered to herself. For her birthday present she'd go to this big place near Columbus, Ohio. She could say she saw Cleveland in the best of times.

When she got into bed she pulled up the scratchy sheets. Sleep. She woke up sweating in the pitch-back darkness, aware that she couldn't breathe. Choking, she tried to scream but only little strangly sounds came out. Clawing at the sheets, blinking her eyes, she tugged at her throat.

Someone or something was trying to kill her.

Not a nightmare. Really happening. She pulled desperately at her neck, cut her fingernails on the rough hands that were trying to strangle her. Couldn't be happening. Not now. Not in the hospital.

The doorway opened. From the little light she saw the upside-down face with the crooked smile and the eyes that had been watching her. The door swung open wide and a big swinging flashlight canvassed the room.

"Everything okay in here?"

B.J. sputtered and the thing with cold hands climbed off her throat so she could breathe again.

"Fine," she said to the matron who came every night and took the count—who was in bed or who wasn't in bed and did someone know why.

"Shit," she said from the small and dark places just behind the lockers.

"Sure?" the light said. "There is extra orange juice at the nurses' station."

B.J. shook her head violently. "No, I'll be fine."

A little later she heard a door being closed lightly and realized it was the killer. So she had to be on the nursing staff. Or maybe snuck in with the laundry cart. No matter. That person wanted to kill her. But why?

THEY had given her the blue shirtwaist dress she had worn at the trial and the sneakers. The dirty, embarrassing sneakers. All of the patients clustered around her in the hall, hugging her and kissing her as if she were leaving the hospital to go home. She knew they didn't really care.

She hadn't been outside in a year. Now when she stumbled down the steps she felt almost dizzy from the air, every little breeze feeling like a gust. The white sunshine blinded her eyes so that she had to squint to see the bus in front of the building. Walking slowly, she wanted to linger in the drowsy sunshine. Who knew when she would get anymore?

She had told the morning shift that the aide with the white hair, tight bun, the one who had told her from the first day that she hated baby-killers, had tried to strangle her. She had been given an aspirin. Bad dream, they said. She was nervous because she was afraid of leaving. This had been her home. She was told she didn't say goodbyes too well. Now she had left and no one would ever know.

"We ain't got all day, lady. The warden don't like dawdlers."

She tripped on a shoelace and stopped to tie it. Looking up at the yellow bus, she took a deep breath. Carrying no suitcase, she climbed on and as she did heard a low whistle. She turned to the bus driver who was sitting at the wheel reading the paper.

There were over ten women sitting scattered in the bus. Most were black, some were Hispanic, and there was one white woman besides herself. She heard it again, a sucking sound, like a puckering kiss. Only it had made her angry. She whirled around again as the bus driver stashed his paper and got ready to start up.

He hadn't done it. But if it wasn't the bus driver, who had made those obscene smacking sounds obviously directed at her to put her in her place? The only other people on the bus were women. That didn't make sense.

WHEN B.J. finally pressed to the window, the first thing she saw were the fences topped with barbed wire. As they came closer she saw that there were also beautiful grounds and, behind a wooded area, a farm. But the view was soon blotted out by the massive orange brick wall of the Ohio Reformatory for Women.

My God, the thought suddenly occurred, she might spend her whole life locked behind those orange bricks. Her face was wet with tears when the bus stopped in front of the penitentiary.

The black woman in front of her turned around. "What you doin' time for, baby?"

B.J. turned around, her hair in her eyes, and looked into the scarred face. The woman smiled back at her. Two of her front teeth were missing, one on her upper lip and another on the bottom lip.

97

*doing time, doing time, that's what it was, really*

"For a crime I didn't do," B.J. cried bitterly, terribly afraid of the big building.

"That's what we all say. But I believes you, girl. Me, baby, I stabbed my old man and I'd do it again, I'll tell you sweetheart, the motherfucker."

As they were being led like cows off the bus, B.J. tried to savor the fresh air and memorize the way the green grass grew in tiny clumps in between the sidewalk. They marched slowly to the door. Doin' time. Doin' time.

Then the black woman turned around. "You better watch your step, little bit. You know, honey, you, you're real purty. You better watch your step."

THEY stood, hands behind their backs, in a neat double line facing the buxom, gray-haired lady who also stood with her hands behind her. "You girls have got to understand one thing. You can do your time easy or hard. Forget the outside world. We have rules here and you follow those rules. We tell you what to eat, when to sleep, when you can pee, and what to think. You break any rules and we'll make your life a miserable hell. Is that understood?"

One of the Puerto Rican woman broke into a flurry of snickers.

"What are you laughing at? I didn't tell you you could laugh."

"Our lives is already hell," the woman blurted out, still snorting with laughter.

She got smacked across the face. "Shut you fuckin' mouth. We don't care what you think. You think what I tell you to think, understand?"

There was not a sound among the prisoners. If anyone had to swallow, they didn't. B.J. was having a hard time breathing.

The women were then marched into a large examining room. A fat, bald man in a dirty white coat, smoking a smelly cigar, looked them over. A matron yelled, "Take off your clothes and put 'em in a pile."

B.J. raised her hand timidly. "What exactly should we take off?"

" 'Take off your clothes' means all your clothes. If you don't know how to strip bare-assed naked, someone will do it for you."

Slowly B.J. began to undress until she was naked. All of the women had done the same thing, some nonchalantly, others more slowly. There were little piles of clothes like anthills all over the floor.

"You," the doctor indicated.

A grossly fat American Indian woman climbed up on the table, put her fat feet in the stirrups and spread her legs.

"You have a venereal disease?" he asked.

One by one they were each asked that question and all of them replied no. Then they were examined. When it was her turn, she turned her face away because of the liquor on his breath, and when he stuck the ice-cold sharp metal instrument way down inside her, she screamed.

When it was over, thankfully, B.J. started to reach down to cover herself with her clothes. The doctor yelled, "Okay, everyone over here. We're going to find all your hiding places."

B.J. looked at a woman who said, "Sample drug bust, baby."

Tears of humiliation were running down B.J.'s face when it was finally all over. Then they were herded from the chilly room, holding their clumps of clothes like bouquets in front of them.

"Shower time, girls. Get it all off. We don't want no lice."

They were pushed into the huge shower, dodging the

harsh spray. Foul-smelling institutional shampoo was passed around.

The towel they handed her was thin as a washcloth, with large holes the size of bullet holes. Still naked, hugging themselves, they were taken to another room where there were stacks of clothing piled high on the shelves. B.J. staggered under the load she had been issued. There were two ugly sacklike jumpers, two blouses, both white, and an institutionally pin-striped bathrobe with the ties clipped off. They issued two pair of panties that looked like men's shorts (to which they all gagged at once), one pair of black oxfords (no half sizes) and a pair of large-sized sneakers, a hairbrush, and a sanitary belt.

In the next room she posed for a picture and they put a number under it. Number 1,012. *Click, click, click.* Next. That would be her name from now on.

"B.J. Stronger?" a corrections officer belted out. B.J. snapped around, her fingertips still black from the fingerprinting.

"Yes? That's me."

"Get moving. You're wanted in the warden's office."

# Chapter Ten

As B.J., puzzled, followed the corrections officer out the door, she received little supportive taps on the arms and back.

"You gettin' out, honey?"

"Been sprung, lucky you!"

Her knees felt weak and she had to force herself to walk. Something had happened. Why would the warden call her alone into his office and no one else?

The warden's secretary buzzed her to enter the office where B.J. and the corrections officer sat down. She looked around. Everywhere were photographs and watercolor paintings of birds. He collected pictures of birds. Then in about ten minutes she was gestured in.

"Have a seat," he said.

He didn't look up.

He opened a file folder and looked up. "Betty Jo Stronger?"

B.J. was biting her fingernails. Why didn't he just tell her she was getting out? That they had finally found she was innocent?

He turned back to his papers as if to verify that. She stared at this big, muscular man. There was a pencil-thin scar running from his left ear to his cheek. He liked to run the tip of his finger over it when he was thinking. A warden in Texas, he had been in a brushfire from a riot. He had asked to be transferred to a woman's prison, thinking it would be an easier job for a man in his fifties. It wasn't.

He looked over the woman sitting in front of his desk. Wide eyes, puckered mouth, baby-soft skin. B.J. Stronger. They didn't often get someone who had made headlines. Men's prisons got most of them. So this was the famous baby-killer. She looked like a baby herself.

"I was asked to tell you in person that your second appeal was denied. Sorry."

He watched the reddish blondish hair fall in front of her face as she studied the floor. He had the queerest urge to brush her hair away from her face as he would for one of his daughters.

When she looked up her eyes were wide, unblinking. "There must be some mistake," she said. She had walked in here thinking she would be free.

"No mistake. Now I see you're going to do nine years to life . . ."

*to life*

". . . and you don't have a previous record."

"I didn't kill that baby, Warden, sir."

He snapped the file folder shut. "But you were found guilty as charged." She was so young. "Listen," he said, leaning back in his chair. "Best I can tell you is to make it easy on yourself. Follow the rules and regulations. There is such a thing as good behavior, you know. Do easy time. You might get out in nine years."

*Might get out in nine years . . .*

"I'll be twenty-seven," she said dully.

"Well," he said, smiling. "That's not so old." He turned to the work on his desk and B.J. realized she was to go. He was finished with her.

But she didn't get up. She pleaded with him. "Please don't let me stay here. I didn't do it. Why would I kill a baby? I wouldn't kill a little baby."

He pressed a button and the door opened. His secretary stood there and beckoned to her that her time was up.

The warden looked up and she was gone. On his desk was a picture of a woman of about twenty-seven with a plump baby on her knee. He traced his scar with his finger. She had been so fresh and sweet-looking, this girl. Pity. She wouldn't stay that way for long.

A key turned with a click and B.J. was led into a cell in Cell Block F. There were two women lying on the bunk bed. Beside it was a makeshift cot, added to cram more women into an already overcrowded prison. There were two tall lockers and a lidless toilet. Cracked and dirty.

"Hi," B.J. said to her two roommates.

They didn't say anything. One of them snorted.

Finally the woman on the top bunk, a wiry black woman with big hands, said, "Hi!" very energetically, a touch of sarcasm in her voice.

On the bottom bunk, a fat, big-busted Hispanic woman who was sucking on her thumb laughed and slapped her thigh.

"Well, now," she said. "What's your name, baby-pants?"

"B.J.," she heard herself say, "B.J. Stronger."

"Ain't that nice," said the woman on the top bunk. "This here's Tough Tits and I'm Bubbles."

"Hey, you look real familiar," Tough Tits said. "Ain't you the bitch who killed that baby? I saw your face plastered all over the TV like you do somethin' special. I got two babies myself somewhere. Don't like baby-killers. Different if I do it to my own but you has to be a mean bitch."

A noise like a foghorn announced the count. B.J. learned they did this five times a day, like a religious ritual. It was automatic and a man sitting in control

103

over the rooms pulled the switches and locked all the doors. Then a guard called off her unit, writing down the numbers in the Control Center. B.J., Bubbles, Tough Tits stood at attention, their arms on the door until they heard "Count clear! Count clear!"

That number sewed to her jumper: 1,012. That's who she was now. When she looked up, it was into the eyes of the other two women who were standing very close.

"What do you think, Mommie?" Bubbles said to Tough Tits.

"Sweet enough to eat. We got a fight on our hands."

She didn't know exactly what they meant but she knew she was blushing. As she sat down on the wobbly cot, she saw something race across the floor. It was a mouse. She started to scream and then felt a hand over her mouth. Bubbles whispered in her ear, "Just shut up, you hear. Or you'll get the hole. Solitary."

All through the dinner of frankfurters, watery mashed potatoes, and half-cooked kernels of corn, as she pushed her fork around her plate, she could feel herself blushing the same way. The women were staring at her, smiling and discussing her, appraising her. She told herself it was her imagination, this thing that was happening, but she knew it wasn't.

After supper, in the Recreation Room, she saw women knitting, sewing, ironing blouses, writing letters, and setting each other's hair in fat rollers. Then she saw a big black woman holding hands with a young prisoner, a woman who looked slightly confused. B.J. looked away, understanding immediately. She had heard about that kind of thing. But she didn't like it. It would never be something she could do.

At ten-thirty, the lights went out in her room.

"Goodnight, Bubbles," she said.

No one said anything.

"Goodnight, Bubbles," she said, again.

"Goodnight, Tough Tits."

It started with a snicker, then B.J. heard the muffled sound of laughter. She lay awake in the dark, staring at the ceiling, thinking prison would be worse than the mental hospital, but she didn't exactly know why.

She never dreamt anymore. It was as if she had shut out that part of her unconscious. But that night she dreamt of her grandparents. They were scolding her, accusing her, telling what a bad, undeserving little girl she was. Her parents stepped out of the coffins and they were protecting her, shielding her. Mother wore ribbons in her hair. Father was tall and handsome. Her grandparents pushed and stuffed them back into their coffins and began to beat and pull her, ripping her clothes.

She struggled out of her bad dream, blinking her eyes open only to find it wasn't a dream. There were harsh and ugly voices in the room. Her nightgown was being ripped. Hands pinched her shoulders and her thighs as they pinned her down to the cot. As her big cotton panties were slid off, B.J. kicked wildly, her legs like scissors, trying to scream for help. A smelly hand covered her mouth, her ankles were shackled with other hands. She looked up into the dim light of a flashlight and saw ten or fifteen women crammed into the cell, eyes and mouths looking down at her.

She was dragged from the cot to the cold floor, naked.

"Let the C.O. in first," someone whispered hoarsely.

Oh, dear God, B.J. thought, if the guards are in on it, who would save her?

Had she thought that before or after someone kicked her hard in the stomach? Half-unconscious, she felt her legs being forced apart until she was spread-eagled on the floor.

"Make a noise, you little cunt, and we'll kill you,"

someone hissed. She tried to nod but couldn't, just as she couldn't make a noise even when she tried.

"Baby, you're going to like it," someone whispered in her ear. But no, no, she knew she wouldn't. She squeezed her eyes shut and told herself this wasn't happening to her. But it was, oh, it was.

The C.O. went first. "Well, we got ourselves a virgin."

B.J. rolled her eyeballs up to the ceiling, past the ceiling and thought she would be sick to her stomach. In the dark shadows of the dimly lit cell she saw only women's legs, hairy legs, and she tried to imagine she was in a forest of trees.

"Guess we should do something about that little predicament," someone said and there was a soft, mean laughter. "No," she pleaded. "No." But it sounded like a wave washing ashore. No one had heard it. No one cared.

She felt the pain first, hideous, humiliating pain. When she opened her puffy eyes she saw the long handle of a broom, grinding, pumping up and down. Tears of rage coarsed down her face and made her eyes burn but she couldn't rub them. The women were silent, watching the strange ceremony. She bit her lip hard, trying to make more pain to take away from this pain.

She prayed she would pass out. Blessed oblivion. She had always thought this would happen with a man, someone she was in love with, but it was a broom. They were raping her with a broom. She turned her head and started to laugh and cry at the same time.

The C.O. jingled a ring of keys. "If you're smart, you'll keep this all to yourself, understand?"

The other women were going back to their cells with her. But B.J. wasn't listening. She couldn't move her right arm at all and her side ached as if all the bones were broken.

The other two women had climbed into bed but B.J. lay on the floor all night, staring into the dark, not blinking. She was lying in a small pool of blood.

She was found in the morning by a guard who rushed in.

"Here, here, get up, get some clothes on. What happened to you?"

B.J. said, in a new voice that surprised her, a harsh, tough voice. "I fell outta bed."

She could see Bubbles open one eye and then close it.

B.J. was taken to the same doctor who had given them internal inspections when they had first come in. He treated her for a sprained arm and a broken rib cage but—he who had probed so deeply looking for a venereal disease—ignored the blood and possible infection. She knew then that she would be punished for it though she was the victim.

THE warden was glaring at her, but she was looking at her shoes.

"You're trying to protect someone. I know you were sexually assaulted by the prisoners. I need to know how they got the key."

B.J. kept her eyes down. He could tell she had a black eye and other bruises; and somehow with all this, which he had predicted, the little-girlishness had vanished. In its place was something else. He couldn't tell what yet.

"I fell outta bed," she said. "I had a bad dream."

"You fell off a cot and broke a rib and sprained an arm."

"Yessir."

"Look," he said, leaning over his desk for emphasis. "The prisoners don't run this place." He stabbed himself in the chest with his thumb. "I do. I need to know what happened and who did it. I'll make sure you're protected."

B.J. said, "I told you, I—"

He interrupted her, sighing. "I know. You fell out of bed."

She watched while the warden stamped some papers and put them in a folder. For the last forty-eight hours she had been in the hole. She had had time to think. It didn't take much brainwork to realize she couldn't be who she was and survive.

"I'll arrange to have you moved to another cell," he said.

"No, that's okay."

"You mean you *want* to go back to the same cell?"

"Yessir."

"Do you think that's . . . wise?"

"Yessir."

He was still shaking his head as B.J. left his office. She was marched down the long corridor to her cell, which was way at the end. The other women were clinging to the bars. They knew. She figured the whole prison knew about the little ceremony. But it would never happen again. She had done too much thinking after she had reached the point where she couldn't cry anymore. She had a plan.

"Hey, baby-pants the baby-killer, a star amongst us," a woman jeered.

"I can do it better than a broom, baby."

"Ain't she sweet!"

But B.J. kept her head held high and kept in step with the C.O., who seemed oblivious to the shouts. It was a joke, she thought. All the good things in life. The kids, her dream of going to New York and making it. Life was filled with the grandmothers of the world.

They violated her with a broom but she would never let anything like that happen again. If she did, she couldn't survive; that was the name of the game in prison.

They had given her shoes that were too big and she stumbled a little to keep up with the silent woman ahead of her. When the cell door unclanked, the two women were lying with their backs toward her on the bunk bed. She sat down on her cot and looked at her old-lady shoes.

"Well, well, look who's done come back home," Bubbles said.

B.J. winced and it made every rib hurt. She took a deep breath and that hurt, too.

"Ain't that nice," Tough Tits said, her round black face shiny under the overhead light.

She knew it was there. Many times she had seen it stuffed under the pillow. Waiting until Bubbles swung down to use the toilet and Tough Tits rolled over, she acted instantly. In one smooth motion, she grabbed the knife and hid it in her underdrawers. Bubbles stood up and flushed and Tough Tits rolled back over. It had happened so fast. B.J. stood there trembling, trying to pretend she wasn't.

That night she lay quietly in her slim cot, waiting. Her hand was in her underpants. The prison was quiet and when she heard them move in the dark she took a deep breath and she was ready.

"Shit, where's my knife?"

"Whaddya mean, where's your knife?"

B.J. pulled the knife out and danced around.

"Hey, what the hell, look at that," Bubbles said. B.J. was holding it up like a sword, still marveling that she had gotten it at all.

Bubbles grabbed for it, and with a strength she didn't know she possessed, the strength of survival, B.J. wrapped her arm around Bubble's neck and aimed the knife at her already-scarred face. Tough Tits grabbed her by her waist, biting her arm until B.J., whimpering, dropped the knife like a hot potato. Then Tough Tits cornered B.J.

Until a voice yelled out, "Drop the goddamned knife!"

It was Bubbles.

# Chapter Eleven

JESSICA Jorrish was not quite two years old when Rachael began to worry that there was something not quite right with the baby. Blond-haired, blue-eyed Jessica had been very carefully selected almost at birth.

"I think there's something wrong with the baby," she said one night to her husband.

Tom put down the paper and lit his pipe. It was natural that his wife would be overly protective, unduly concerned with this baby after what happened to Joshua.

"What's wrong, Rachael?"

His wife looked away. Just yesterday she had seen a woman in Shaker Square who had looked like *her*. But of course she was in prison so that couldn't have been her. But the headaches had started. She had strange dreams of suffocating or sticking or shooting the girl who had killed her baby. Jail wasn't good enough.

Tom had hoped her new psychiatrist would help her out of the slump but it hadn't brought back the old Rachael. Instead, he was married to this prescription junkie who was afraid of the space outside her door and rarely went out.

Finally she blurted it out. "She doesn't talk."

"Well, give her time. She's only two. Some children are slow."

"Josh . . . Joshua . . ." She brushed her now-graying hair out of her eyes. She had forbidden herself to say his name. The psychiatrist wanted her to throw away her obsession and forget now. They had talked about it over and over.

"What else, Rachael?"

"There's something wrong with her, Tom. She's not . . . sweet."

Tom shrugged as if it didn't matter and went back to his newspaper. But he knew perfectly well what Rachael meant. There was something different about that baby. But then, nothing compared to his boy. That baby had been perfect from the very beginning. This baby wasn't quite right when you stopped to think about it. On the other hand, no one would want to take this baby away from them. Especially if it was damaged.

SHE wiped her eyes when the tears started to sting her eyelashes. B.J. was chopping onions. Sitting on a stool, her legs spread wide apart, was Bubbles. Their jobs were to make the dinner, dish it out, and clean up afterwards. They stole as much food as they could. Apples and oranges were slipped inside their blouses and hard-boiled eggs were tucked into their socks. The kitchen was privileged and Bubbles had pulled some strings so B.J. could be there.

Suddenly Bubbles laughed out loud. B.J. wiped the tears from her eyes.

"What's so funny?"

"You. I was rememberin' the night you had me by the neck with that knife. Lord, you've changed since then."

"So what else is new?" B.J. said. Only her new dream, now a dream of revenge. On the murderer of that baby, if it took her a lifetime to find, if she had a life. And on uppity Rachael Jorrish for saying all those ugly things about her that went into the papers. And on the kids, oh yes—they had liked and then they had left her. This dream of revenge nourished her, kept her going.

Since that night with the knife, Bubbles had never given her a reason for her unconditional protection. In the yard where they got a precious few minutes of sunshine, she had been threatened sexually by old Fat Florence, surrounded by her entourage of followers.

"Gonna have you transferred into my cell, baby. Show you a real good time." And she had meant it, too. Next to Bubbles, Fat Flo was the leadership of the prison inmates. B.J. had stared at her yellowish crooked teeth and the mean smile until Bubbles had pulled her away.

"Lay off or I'll kill you," she had told Fat Florence and marched the trembling B.J. away.

"Why did you do it?" It had been on her mind for so long. The scrawny, tough black woman had taken care of her and never laid a hand on her.

There was no answer except the methodical scraping of potatoes and the thump as the peelings hit the pail. "Well, let's just say I like your stuff, girl. Liked the way you stood up to all of us that night. That took guts. You somethin' special, girl. Fine. You don't deserve this place. Now shaddup and don't ask no more questions."

B.J. watched out of the corner of her eye as some women were making off with a pile of steaks that had been set aside for the warden and other prison officials. They would take anything that wasn't nailed down and so would she. Why should the warden eat steaks and lobster while they ate franks and lima beans?

Bubbles leaned in toward her and her voice was soft for Bubbles: "There's a contract out on you."

B.J. put down her onion for a second and felt a familiar sinking inside. "What does that mean?"

"Someone is waiting to ice you right here in the slammer. Heard it through prison grapevines."

"But that couldn't happen here." B.J. left off the rest of her sentence: Could it?

Bubbles laughed. "Oh, sure that sort of thing happens in jail. But it's hushed. You don't find much about it in the newspapers, because nobody's talkin', you see what I mean? Stabbings, stranglings. They set it up so it looks like a suicide. Prisoner died because of depression. Didn't like the food." She laughed again.

B.J. shuddered. "But why would any of the prisoners—"

"Not here, baby, not here," Bubbles interrupted solemnly. "On the outside. Someone who thinks prison won't do the job. Someone who wants to make sure you never get a chance to do life and is willing and rich, and able to pay for it."

"It's Fat Florence, isn't it?"

Bubbles put down her skinned potato. "She just wants your pussy. Matter of power. Her issue is with me, honey, not with you.'Course she'll kill you when she's finished with you. But you ain't goin' in that cell. Long as Bubbles is around, ain't nothin' goin' to happen and she knows it."

B.J. just kept on chopping onions and trying to understand it all. Her job paid $1.75 and she needed the money to buy what she needed in prison. She shut her burning eyes and remembered her last night in the hospital, the tightness around her neck as that woman had tried to kill her.

Maybe she wasn't crazy. Maybe the killer was paying money to see that she wasn't alive too long.

She picked up another smelly onion and realized she was terrified. Bubbles would be maxing out. She would have done her extra time and she would be leaving. She pictured Fat Florence's rotting teeth, the knife she kept tucked in her shorts, the knife she had said she would use to carve a little tattoo on B.J.'s face with her big hands, big as a man's. She had nightmares about the woman.

And now there was someone she couldn't picture who was being paid to kill her. She shook her head and the tears she brushed way weren't only from the sting of the onions.

Without Bubbles's protection, her life wasn't worth shit.

THE women lined up as the matron quickly inserted her rubber-gloved hand from front to back as the women stood naked. Standard procedure before going into the visiting room and coming out. B.J. stood red-faced and humiliated, wondering why Mort had come once again and if she ever wanted to see him again.

But when she went out into the visiting room she saw it wasn't Mort.

"Debbie? Debbiieee!" she shrieked.

Debbie stood up and hugged and kissed her old friend. She was wearing a navy skirt and white-collared top and was unmistakably pregnant.

"Beej, you look wonderful as always! How's the food in this place?"

She looked at Debbie and in the back of her mind, she felt a twinge of anger. Was that all she could say? Then she remembered that Debbie had come all this way to see her and indicated her thin gold wedding band and protruding stomach.

"I see you didn't do so bad for yourself," B.J. said, smiling.

"I married Frankie, Beej. We tried to have a baby for the longest time and now look. Isn't it funny how things turn out?"

B.J. wanted to scream—why didn't you visit me in

the hospital, why didn't you write, why did you say what you did at the trial—but of course she couldn't. She realized then that Debbie thought she was looking at the old B.J., couldn't know that she had changed, oh, so much.

"How are all the kids?" she asked stiffly.

"Oh, honey, forget about that," Debbie said, brushing her hair with her hand. "The Summers are long done gone and the Townies they got big bellies and bills. Most of 'em stayed in Madison."

B.J. stared at her, watching her mouth and wondering what shade of red lipstick she was wearing. Debbie's mother had never let her wear lipstick.

"Saw your brother, Wilton, looking all spruced up in a suit and a tie. He sold us a car from his lot. In fact, Wilton has been very successful. He owns some real estate in Madison and . . ."

She wasn't listening. Just watching the red lips. She didn't want to hear about Wilton, to learn the half-wit was cleaning up. Had he ever come for a visit?

"What about Hughie?"

Debbie stopped in mid-sentence and took a breath.

"Hughie? Well, let's see. He went to Harvard, goin' on to law school or in it and he wants to go into politics. Got the looks for it. He's doing real good but that's just gossip. We never see him no more."

Taking a deep, almost raspy breath, B.J. said very carefully, "Why did he lie under oath at my trial?"

Debbie looked down and seemed to get angry. "Aw, Beej, we don't want to hash over all that stuff. I'm not sure he did lie, now. You knew Hughie. He liked to joke around. But maybe he wasn't there that night."

Maybe. But he was on her revenge list.

"But I thought we'd have a pleasant little visit and then I'd get back on that bumpy little bus and feed my Frankie if we get home in time."

She didn't even say "Frankie says hello."

116

There was an embarrassing silence. B.J. felt as if she were being strangled the same way she had that night. She was doing ten years to life and Debbie was telling her that Hugh liked to joke around?

B.J. started to cry. Debbie reached over, patted her on the knee and murmured, "Now, honey, don't get yourself all excited, you know Hugh's family background. It would be an awful mess if he got himself in trouble."

As soon as she had started, the tears dried up and she felt ashamed of herself. "Debbie," she asked. "Do you think I killed that baby?"

Her old friend didn't answer for a moment and then she said, a half-smile on her face, "Now, honey, don't be thinkin' 'bout things like that. Of course I don't think you killed that baby." She stood up. "But I'm glad we had a chance to chat. When this baby comes I'll be real busy."

She watched Debbie walk out and then saw her cross herself. Debbie only did that when she thought she had committed some kind of mortal sin. Like lying. So Debbie thought she had done it. Then all the kids thought she was guilty. Then she knew why Debbie had come. It was a good omen for the baby, a good-thing to do. Something that resembled a lucky charm for the child.

Walking slowly back to the room behind the Visitor's Room, she knew a part of her was gone forever. There were no more kids. Everything had changed. She stripped bare and waited for the feel of the rough hand. But instead she got the softest of love taps. Rigidly she straightened up, her knees shaking. Had that been the touch of the woman hired to kill her?

Bubbles lay on the top bunk, her arms behind her head, knees up, white socks against thin black legs, blowing bubbles from the ever-present bubble gum she chewed.

"Well, she just a bitch, baby, forget her. Forget them. What they ever done for you?"

"They were my friends," B.J. said.

Bubbles fingered a love note passed from another inmate through B.J. She picked the purple bubble gum out of her mouth and pulled it into a long string. Then she popped it back into her mouth.

"Remember that dream of yours? Well, that's just about the nicest dream I ever did hear. And maybe you can still do it, who knows?"

"Oh, that would be impossible," B.J. answered.

"Well, fix it up a bit, you know. Keep it a top priority. Tell me. Tough Tits is done doing her time. But I'll tell ya, honey. With friends like that, baby, you don't need no enemies. That's what my old man says."

"You have a boyfriend, Bubbles?"

"Of course and he'd kill for me, sugar, because I'm the only one that gives him what he needs."

"But . . ."

Bubbles laughed and put the ball of purple gum inside her love letter. "Oh, that. We all do it, honey. Gotta have a little lovin' but it don't mean nothing to most of us. Now, listen, you stop crying. Your friends are in here."

B.J. thought of the murderer who was trying to kill her. Which friend was it? She thought of it in the mess hall, in the showers, where sex went on all the time, when she was marched down the corridor and into the yard. If Bubbles had a knife, so could any of the others. Fat Florence kept one in her man's size shorts. Even with Bubbles around, she felt she could never rest. She never felt safe.

When Bubbles left, she would probably be moved to Fat Florence's cell and raped every night. But no one dared to make a move while Bubbles was still there. The warden had been wrong. It was the prisoners who ran the prison and who had the power.

"Why don't you take a little nap? Rest yourself."

B.J. shut her eyes, longing for a way out of the depression and hurt, wanting to put Debbie and the rest of the kids as far away as they really were. She must have been asleep less than a half hour when she woke up to loud shrieking. Half asleep, dazed, she could barely make out what all the commotion was about.

"She's dead!" someone shouted and the message went on down from cell to cell.

B.J. sat up and knocked her head on the bottom of the top bunk. Rubbing the sore spot, blinking her eyes, she understood immediately.

One of the prisoners had been murdered.

# Chapter Twelve

THE foghorn went off.

The count began.

It wasn't until she was in the dining room dishing out the food that she heard the gossip. She dropped a lump of wet mashed potatoes on the floor.

"It was Fat Florence!"

"Fat Florence? Who was it she disposed of?"

B.J. skidded on the mashed potatoes on the floor. It had been a mistake. It was Fat Florence who was hired to kill her and she had made a mistake. The next time it would be her.

"Keep it down! Keep it moving," a C.O. roared.

"No, you got it all wrong," someone whispered. "It was Fat Flo who got it." Two women got into a fight over it, one slapping the other one with a dried-out piece of pork until a C.O. broke it up.

But the truth was Fat Florence's body had been hauled out of her cell by three men and the story was she had been depressed. The grapevine had it that she had been stabbed.

B.J. wiped the sweat off her forehead. There was only one other woman in that prison who could have pulled that off.

\* \* \*

SHE liked to tick off the days on the calendar she kept by her bunk with a red pencil. It was said there are no clocks in prison, only calendars. She had given up on Mort or appeal a long time ago but she always needed to know how much more time she was doing.

Bubbles was on the top bunk chewing a wad of strawberry bubble gum. Her arms were wrapped around herself and she was singing a spiritual.

"My oh my, aren't we the happy one?" B.J. said. "It wouldn't be because you were the one behind all this commotion and are just resting with your bubble gum. You killed her, didn't you?"

More cracking and the pop of a broken bubble.

"Wouldn't go that far, sugar."

"Well, then . . . ?"

"We paid off the C.O., so Fat Florence could have a little accident. Actually she tripped and fell on her knife. Always was a clumsy bitch, if you ask me."

"But how did you pay off the guards?" B.J. asked, aware that her voice was high, almost childlike.

She could picture Bubbles lying on the top bunk, smiling, eyes closed. "Like I says, honey, I got friends in high places. My old man's got plenty of dough."

B.J. sat up in the lower bunk and talked to the bottom of the mattress as if she could see through. "But why, Bubbles, why did you take that chance? You could have been killed, you could have lost your parole."

"Baby-pants, she was gonna make mashed potatoes out of you. You would have been her sex slave and she would have carved it all over your pretty face and body with that knife of hers. And then she woulda killed you. All to show me. Even if I was on the outside. Power, that's what counts in this joint. And then she would have collected the cash, you see?"

So it had been her all along. B.J. stared at her calendar. Part of September was slashed out with diagonal

121

bloodred marks. So that meant three and a half months left until 1985. Bubbles would be gone by then.

Who would take care of her?

THE warden's wife had passed away and his daughter, Margaret, had moved in with him in the cozy little cottage on the grounds. She was divorced and had a two-and-a-half-year-old little boy, Mark, named after the warden.

Margaret asked her father for an assistant. She had decided to go into a catering business for herself.

B.J. was picked. She was white, she was attractive, she was clean, and she had kept out of trouble. In the morning she did her prison job. Every afternoon she would run through the fresh fields to another world.

In a way it reminded her vaguely of another time in her life when she had felt contented and happy. When she had been a part of a family. It had been the Jorrishes.

Margaret was tall and slim with her red hair packed into a hair net. B.J. was constantly tripping over Mark, who trundled around the kitchen, stooping to take pots and pans out of the shelves, but she loved him around her.

Margaret taught her how to bake carrot cakes, zucchini cakes, banana bread, how to cook and plan and, finally, how to walk out the door with trays covered with Saran Wrap ready to go. Everything she could learn about the catering business, she learned from Margaret. Not that it would ever help her much.

She wrote Bubbles a letter about her new prison job and Bubbles, who couldn't write, had someone else write to caution her not to trust them folks. Them folks could get her into trouble.

But B.J. had let a little happiness in and she wasn't willing to let it go. She loved the white thatched-roof cottage and the winding driveway that curled into neatly rounded shrubs. Her day started when she broke free from her prison job and stepped into this other world, safe and decent and quiet. Margaret never treated her like a prisoner.

They were taking a batch of cakes out of the oven, one dark, blowy afternoon when they heard the baby crying.

"Beej," Margaret said, "could you just run up and see what's the matter with Mark?"

The rain was pelting the sides of the house when B.J. ran up the stairs, for some reason taking them two at a time. The baby had wakened from his afternoon nap. But when she came to the door of his little blue room she stopped. Mark had stopped his angry crying. She crept up to the side of the little junior bed filled with stuffed animals and saw how still and pale he looked.

His mouth was open, his eyes were open, but he wasn't breathing.

She looked around desperately for a way to escape, a window to climb down. A chance to get away. It was happening again. Oh God, it was happening again. She looked down at the dead baby and, falling to her knees, screamed, "Damn you, wake up!"

As she heard her own voice, she began to lose control of where she was. Margaret, downstairs, heard the scream, dropped a dish of butter on the floor and raced up the stairs. When she reached the child's room she found B.J. crouched like a hunted animal in the corner, rocking, sobbing and waiting.

"Baby's dead. Oh, God, please believe me. I didn't kill the baby. Someone must have come in through the window, climbed up and then . . . killed . . . Joshua . . ."

"B.J., the window's closed. There's no one there. His name is Mark."

"He's dead. I didn't do it." She was pressed to the

doorway with her hands over her face, her hair falling down from its bun.

"Mommy?"

Margaret picked up the little boy. "B.J., are you okay? There's nothing wrong."

B.J. slumped over. The baby was alive. She had been tricked. "I saw everything all over again. The rain. Running up the steps. He was so still. Too still. And everyone thought I did it."

Margaret put her son back in his bed and quickly went to the young woman she had grown so fond of in the last months. She held her gently. "You didn't kill that baby, did you, B.J.?"

"No, oh God, no. I'm innocent. I was always innocent. How could I kill a little baby. There was a killer and they let him get away. But no one believes me."

"Well, I believe you," the warden's daughter said softly. "I believe you, B.J., I believe you."

SHE laughed to herself. He was dressed impeccably in a pin-striped suit with a red silk handkerchief in his pocket. Mort had come to visit her at the tail end of her ninth year.

He stared at the lovely young woman who had matured behind bars. As always there was the scratchiness in the back of his throat whenever he saw her, more so now. Over the years he had not doubted so much the way he handled the trial; rather, lately, before dawn, he debated whether she hadn't told a lie because she was mentally unbalanced. It was easier for him to sleep well, if it was perhaps the case that she was, in fact, guilty.

"Well, you're coming up for parole, B.J.," he said.

She held her breath until she couldn't suck in her stomach any longer.

"I guess after all these years that must look very

124

attractive to you. But I came because in all the years we appealed, I guess I got your hopes up, didn't I?''

She nodded.

"Truth is, Beej, I don't think a parole is likely to happen now. Probably be denied. You'll most likely have to wait a few years. Didn't want you to get your hopes up, you understand?''

"I understand.''

"I came because it seemed the fair and decent thing to. It seems you've gotten your hopes up on those appeals.''

"I understand.''

She studied him. He had grown a mustache. It was black but his hair was turning gray. Parole—she had dreamed of it, spun fantasies about it. But he must know it would be denied. Mort, after all, wasn't some baggie-pants lawyer. He must be on the inside. Sadly she shook hands with him.

IN her cell, she ticked off another day on her calendar, then fell facedown on the top bunk, which was hers. It was late sticky summer and she had a feeling the air outside might be a shade cooler than it was in her cell. She slammed a fly angrily with the back of her hand. She would be here for life then, that was what would happen. Where had the old dream gone? What was it? That she took a suitcase up the long Lake Road to North Madison and she flagged down the bus. And then what? Why, she hadn't been there for ten years. She could never be an actress now. She couldn't stand anyone looking at her. She looked down at the name tag sewn into her limpish jumper.

Her name? No. Her number: 1,012. That was her name now. B.J. stared at the woman through the bars. For a second she didn't understand. Visiting hours were over.

"Warden wants to see you, toot sweet, tootsie.''

She climbed down from the bunk and made the final ten-inch jump to the floor with a thud. This was it. She would sit there and listen to him drone on about her parole being denied. As she followed the C.O. down the corridor, she remembered the first visit to his office when he told her the appeal had been turned down and she had been expecting him to open the door and set her free forever. Those days were long gone, about ten years long gone. She remembered now he had tried to force her to say she had been raped and how Bubbles had informed her that she would have been "dead meat" if she had.

Sitting across from Warden O'Brian she looked at his yellowish whitish hair and red pockmarked face, and saw little Mark. Actually she thought he looked more like a priest or a minister. All he needed was stained-glass windows. She pictured going along the sand by the shore and picking up water-smoothed little pieces of glass. The American flag looked a little dusty but other than that, everything was the same. Even the way he had of not looking up but shuffling a sea of papers around on his desk. She was looking out the window when he did and seemed to hear the words long after they had been spoken: "Your parole has been granted. You're free."

AFTER ten years she was free. Free to smell the air, free to eat all the junk food she had seen on television, free to look at a square space without bars in front of her. She would be free of the constant sounds of sex in the showers, through the cell bars. She was a free woman. With one dream: to make everyone who had made her suffer pay for it.

First she'd have to find the killer.

Then she'd find a way to hurt smug rich-boy Hughie.

After that she'd make Debbie and the rest of the kids feel like she had been made to feel.

Then there was Rachael Jorrish. Somehow she would make her take back all those things she had told the press that had slanted the trial and given her the image of a crazed murderess.

It would be sweet.

She thought only of her plan to kill the killer.

THEN they were in the yard being marched around. It was early fall. But the one oak tree in the yard was fussed on because it was the only tree, and each prisoner wanted to think the tree belonged to them. It was under that tree that she heard the voice: "Don't turn around or you'll be playing with my knife."

At first she thought it was Fat Flo, but she was dead a few years ago. She felt the blade and the woman said, "Look, I'm going to push a large packet into your dainty little pants. And I don't want you to open it until you hit your bunk."

B.J. moved and felt the cold paper of the envelope crumple beneath the elastic of her rubber waistband.

"Now get outta here, sister, and mum's the word."

B.J. looked at it under the covers when lights were out. It was money—a lot. B.J. had mentally figured it all out, marveling at Bubble's resources. Two thousand dollars in one-hundred-dollar bills. This woman who she would probably never see again had just changed her world. What she got out of prison was forty dollars and that's it. The note was made of cutout letters and the message was loud and clear:

Don't go after no revenge, baby.
Revenge ain't sweet.
No, baby, you never get anything out of it but heartache and hell. You don't belong in this joint so forget about it. Remember Bubbles.
I know. Be sweet. Bubbles.

127

The last word had a child blowing bubbles from a wand. She looked at her calendar with the red slashes. Pretty soon.

Was Bubbles right?

# BOOK

# III

# Chapter Thirteen

B.J. looked around. "I'll take it," she said to the landlady, Mrs. Panny.

"Sure. Need a pen?"

"No, I have one here," she said a little too quickly.

B.J. had picked a dot on the map. Salem, Ohio. Not too far from the prison in Southern Ohio. Ohio University was nearby and that would be great for her plans. Also she was far away but not too far.

"I'm going to open up a little catering business. Call it 'Gourmet to Go.'" On the cement wall were hooks with cooper pots and pans. B.J. pulled out a drawer and saw it was filled with utensils. The cabinets held faded green glass dishes, though they were a little dusty.

"I guess this place needs a real scrub-down," B.J. said.

Mrs. Panny decided to lower the rent. Apparently the girl had asked around and knew the story.

"Well, like I says, the place needs a little airing. You can have it for $175 a month. Call me if you need anything."

B.J. calculated what she had left in the envelope from Bubbles. She had bought a secondhand van for six hundred dollars and then had picked up some clothes at a discount place. "It'll be perfect," she said firmly. She needed to get to work.

"Okay, then, it's settled. Now if you will write a check to—"

"Oh," B.J. said, somewhat alarmed. "I don't have a check. Will you accept cash?"

Mrs. Panny turned and looked at the girl over the skinny glasses that had fallen down to her big nose. "Cash would be fine, dear," she said. Nobody paid cash nowadays unless they had just robbed the nearest gas station. Which was ridiculous. Something slightly unusual about this girl. But it was really none of her business.

She took the money, noticing the large envelope and said nothing except "Don't want no trouble here. No wild parties, no . . . why, I don't even know your name."

Name. Why hadn't she thought of that? She looked around at the beginnings of a new life and, looking down at a newspaper yellow with age, picked a new one: "Barbara Marshall," she said, not even having time to select what she wanted.

"Well, then, Miss Marshall, I'll see you again on October first for the rent."

As she walked back to her car, she thought maybe she could have gotten away with security. She just wasn't real sure how much the girl knew about that old house. If she pressed her luck, she wouldn't have a tenant at all.

B.J./Barbara stood outside the door and tried to remember the last time she had felt happy. She wasn't quite sure of the feeling. But she thought this was coming close. Yes, it just might be.

She had spent ten years half-alive. Well, no one would stop her from living again. She got into her van and drove off to find a discount drugstore. She had changed her name to Barbara. But that wasn't enough.

132

* * *

SHE pulled the towel away slowly. But she could tell through the wet tangle of hair what she had. Number 36. Moonbeam Flaxen blond. She parted her shoulder length hair in the middle, not quite believing it at first. Blond and Barbara.

Whistling while she worked, she scrubbed down the kitchen, so she could start working. Margaret had taught her everything that she needed to know about the catering business.

Before it got dark, she decided to walk around the grounds. In the back was a thick, brambly blackberry patch whose ripe fruit could be made into pies.

She was taking a break looking over her blackberry patch, thinking, wearing a large straw hat and blue shorts and a white top.

"Hey," someone yelled. "A penny for your thoughts."

B.J. swung around and saw a man struggling with the starter of a power mower. "You the new tenant?"

She nodded and he came over, extended his hand, and then pumped hers. "I'm Leroy Phillips. Retired history professor from the university. What are you doing in the boring town of Salem?"

She smiled, hanging over her picket fence. "Oh, I have a little catering business. Thought I'd pick up some in the university."

"Lots of business there, sure," he said. He wore a turned-down sailer cap, sideways. He reached under the cap to scratch his head. "If you plug in the right network you should do a big service. Have you got one of those answering machines?"

She looked confused. "I never saw one."

"More and more people are using those things for social reasons but it's just the thing for your business. I have one and I'm not anybody right now. It's just

133

convenient. Come in my house a minute and I'll show you how it works.''

She let him lead her to his house, almost identical to her house. All the venetian blinds were drawn and there was a floor fan grinding away.

"What is it?" B.J. said and suddenly wished she hadn't.

He gave her an odd look.

It looked like a tape recorder. There was a red light like a fish eye.

"Now, when I get in and there's a message, this here light blinks on and off. Like a little heartbeat." B.J. backed a little bit to get a better distance. The man had been drinking and the smell of his breath was more noticeable in the small foyer.

"Then I press this button that says REWIND and then I hit PLAY. Like this."

She listened as the voice filled the room like a radio. She had never seen one and she realized that there were many things she had missed being locked up for years. Ten years had gone by. No one in Madison had had one. But now they probably did. But what bothered her was she had never had a phone before. And that mistake. She would have to be careful not to make too many slips like that.

Leroy, enjoying himself, pressed the FAST FORWARD button. "It takes up to twenty messages," he said, satisfied with himself.

But there was something about it she just didn't like. It was so impersonal. She knew for sure she would be tongue-tied if she ever had to talk into one of those things. That machine was definitely something she couldn't afford. Besides she would mostly be at home, baking.

"Want a gin and tonic?" he asked impetuously. "On a hot day like this you could use something with a little zip to it, somethin' real icy."

134

She shrugged. "Lemonade will be fine." Oh well, he was her next-door neighbor. A lot of the women had had a drinking problem. The most B.J. had ever drunk was half a beer at the Bluebird Inn. This Leroy probably was into the bottle a lot more. She looked at her watch.

Leroy Phillips came in with two glasses. There was the smell of fresh-cut green grass. They were just around the corner from fall and she would see the foliage, which she barely remembered.

They had their feet up on television tables.

"Why did you rent that house next door?"

"I liked the kitchen," she replied simply, then she realized how stupid that sounded.

"You renting the top or the bottom?"

"No one lives upstairs," she answered, wondering now why she hadn't asked more questions. "Why?"

"There's something wrong with that house, little lady," he whispered and B.J. had to lean in to get the words straight. "The house has gone unrented for near five years, that's why I was surprised to see you there. The house is haunted."

B.J. giggled and then put her hand over her mouth as if she were stifling a hiccup.

He turned to her with such a look of reproval, she came close to apologizing. "There was once a shooting in that house. A man killed his wife and then ran into the yard, apparently berserk, or that's how the papers printed it. With the same gun, he shot himself through the heart and then crawled slowly up the steps. Some say he lived for a short while."

It was still in the early twilight, except for a cricket singing somewhere in a bush.

"Do you exactly believe that?"

Leroy laughed. "Well, take a look out back. Place was left untended for years. No one wanted to rent it.

Kids played in it. It more than earned its reputation as haunted house.''

B.J. smiled and shook her head, but his telling of it had frightened her because he was scared.

"Well," he said, "take a look out back. All those blackberry brambles crawling up the back of the house. Place was left untended for years. No one did anything before you came here. Now I want to know the real story.''

She stood up and her legs felt like wobbly colt's legs.

His smile, when he chose to show it, looked like he was amusing himself. The sandals, the pull-over sweater, and his jeans made him look like a professor— or what she thought a professor should look like. But he was making her uncomfortable. She was never good around men.

"Thanks for the tip," she said. He began to laugh and laugh.

"What's so, funny?" B.J. said.

He shrugged and then nodded. "Don't rightly know. Don't really know what lived there, but that's for you to change.''

"I don't have a key for the upstairs," she said. But she did have the key to upstairs. She ran to her little house, one-half kitchen and the other contained space. She wasn't going to do anything about it. Bubbles used two mottos: *Screw it and do it* and *When in doubt, do nothing.* She wished she could talk to Bubbles and some of the other girls. But she knew she had to be a shade less friendly. Never trust the neighbors, Bubbles also had conveyed to her in her note.

Tomorrow she would start baking carrot and zucchini cakes and she'd drive down to the valley near where the professors and their wives were. They would want catered luncheons. As far as her knowledge and research of this spot went, there weren't any other caterers for miles around.

That night she hugged the soft pillow to her chin and stared at the ceiling. She had never slept all alone before. They had been three to a cell and before that had been her grandparents' house. And before that . . . and before that. She rolled over, willing herself to think of something else. The blackberries outside the house, large and ripe—maybe she could bake a pie.

Taking the covers with her, she shot straight up in bed.

There was a noise, like a door slamming.

Rigid, afraid to blink, she heard another noise. That of a low, mournful moan. Sliding slowly out of bed, she ran into the dark kitchen, fumbled frantically for what she thought was the right drawer and pulled out a long kitchen knife. Pinning herself flat against the wall again, she heard the slamming noise. Looking wildly around, the knife clenched between her teeth, she ran on her heels to the little bedroom, where she crawled under the bed, trembling helplessly.

The creaking groan again.

Maddening silence.

A dog barked from somewhere.

There was another angry slam.

For a minute, a silly thought ran through her mind—she could dash next door. Instead, she breathed as softly as she could. And that's how she finally fell asleep. Hiding under the bed with a huge knife for protection. She had not had that much sleep. It was almost a surprise to see the morning. She crawled out from under the bed and crept barefoot, in her nightgown, all around the small house. Nothing was out of place. The only sounds she had heard were the music of the country outside her windows.

When she was tucking her sheets into careful hospital corners, she saw the knife gleaming, picking up the rays of early morning sunlight, and vowed that this would never happen again. Nothing and no one would ever make her follow their voices. She wouldn't live like that. It would mean she was still a prisoner. It was safe now. It was morning. Outside, two thrushes were singing.

Carrying the knife for protection, she marched herself out the door and up the steps that led to the empty space above her. She found the door unlocked, slightly ajar. Silently, she stuck her toe in the door and saw white everywhere. She closed her eyes. Ghosts wore white, didn't they? Opening the door just an inch or two more, she saw dirty white sheets covering chairs and a sofa.

Dust got up her nose and she sneezed twice. When she did that there was a shaking somewhere high in the wooden beams. She ducked as a big, black bat circled the room, its wings flapping busily.

Screaming, she buried her head in her arms and shouted, "Shoo, go away!"

The slamming noise. She saw a broken shutter waving in the wind. The ugly bat had probably nose-dived into things, like some drunken pilot. So that was the upstairs. Haunted. Sure it was. She smiled to herself. Maybe the ghosts didn't come out in the daytime.

She made a mental note to tell the landlady there was a bat upstairs and ask her to secure the shutter, then she ran down the steps and put the silly knife away.

Leroy was standing on the other side of the fence waving when she came out of the kitchen door, in pants and a top.

"Nice day, isn't it?" he said. There was a bottle of gin at his feet.

"Looks like."

"Where are you going?"

She waved the little batch of fliers that she had drawn. Why did he want to know that?

"Because you can have them Xeroxed."

"Where?"

"Main Street, where else? Next door to the newspaper that fella runs."

"Oh, I was going to go there. But they look better this way. Each one is a little different."

"Okay, then. Say, how much were you able to sleep last night?"

B.J. stopped and slowly turned around. Why did he want to know that?

"Oh, there were some noises in the house. It was nothing. Found a bat upstairs."

"Well, listen to me. You're a newcomer. We don't get many of those. What you need is 'Ghostbusters.' "

"What's that?" she said and then shut her mouth. She had done it again. He shrugged as if she was in the right by not knowing.

"It's just a movie, very funny, with Dan Akroyd."

"Oh, that. Of course I know *Ghostbusters*. Only I never saw it."

"Oh, sure," he said. She ran to her old van and started it up, backing out of the grassy driveway, watching the man with his turned-down sailor hat watching her. He seemed always to be watching her. But then again, she wasn't used to being neighborly.

Leroy scratched his shining hair underneath his hat and smiled. He couldn't even control his facial muscles anymore so he didn't even feel the corners of his mouth turn up.

There was something awesome about that girl. Mighty strange behavior. As if she'd been on another planet for a few years. He turned toward his house, sniffing. Well, he'd find out. That's what people did in this town. Everybody had a weak spot somewhere when you brought it out of hiding.

# Chapter Fourteen

It took an hour to get to the outlying section of Athens that she wanted. Parking her van, she grabbed her fliers and a roll of tape. It was a quiet little community and she stopped for a moment to cross her fingers. A bicycle whizzed by and she saw a young mother wheeling a baby carriage. The college would be opening soon for early registration. This was the best place to start.

Methodically she went from trees to telephone poles, slicking down a piece of tape and smoothing it down. She stood back and read one: "Gourmet-to-Go." She liked the name. And the little drawing of a van with wings. That was a nice touch.

"That's weird," a voice said. A little boy of about eleven or twelve came up to her.

"What's weird?"

"Because my mom said she was looking for something like this. My sister's getting engaged and we have to have this party. So she needs someone to do the food and stuff, you know?"

He squinted up at her in the sunshine and B.J. felt her heart flutter, if hearts did such a thing. She handed him a flier and pointed to her phone number.

"When can she call you?"

"Oh, anytime. I'm there. Cooking and baking."

As she finished her postering and found her van, she realized something. What if his mother called when she was out? She would lose her first job. When she had worked for Margaret, there had never been this problem.

She or someone else had done all the errands and deliveries. She grabbed her envelope and counted and recounted the money. Leroy was right. She had no other choice but to get one of those dreadful little answering machines.

"New to town?"

"The cheapest one you've got."

He pulled out a little black boxlike thing: "It's $79.95. You just plug it in. See those little red strips? When the top one kind of beeps on and off, silently of course, you press the silver bar and it rewinds and automatically plays your message."

She counted out the twenties and tens in her envelope and then looked up at the youngish clerk. He seemed to be appraising her. He put the box in a bag, stapled the receipt to the top and said perfunctorily, "I'm sure you'll be happy with this machine."

"I'm sure I'll hate it," she found herself saying and rushed out of the store.

That afternoon when she was following the maddening directions, plugging in the machine, squeezing it in on top of the little telephone table, she thought of the night ahead of her. She told herself that it would be easier to sleep, that she would sleep on top of the bed and not under it. She smiled. She knew what all the noises were now. She stood there studying her machine and shook her head, looking up at the ceiling, biting her lip, feeling the panic of the night before. What had caused the floorboards to creak upstairs?

\* \* \*

THE newspaper slid off her knees and fell to the floor. It couldn't be true. It was impossibly maddening to believe it, but she was free! Where was justice? They had parolled her. Whose baby was she going to kill now?

Rachael Jorrish put her coffee mug down on the end table, watching a pool of muddy coffee slosh all over the glass. Stumbling like a blind person, she opened every drawer in the mahogany cabinet until she found what she was looking for. An old crumpled pack of Salem Lights lay in a corner underneath some cloth napkins. Rachael inhaled one thankfully, then immediately felt dizzy from the stale cigarette.

Quickly she folded up the *Plain Dealer*. Tom couldn't see this. He would be furious, incensed. Ten years. Had she really been that other Rachael who had everything? Until it was taken away from her. And Tom. His hair was almost complete gray now and he was as handsome as he was then. Tom shouldn't see this, not the way she had. She remembered his breakdown a year or two after Joshua had . . . had gone away. Together they walked the halls together, smoking, talking, coloring in kid's coloring books, talking until Tom was Tom again. Tears of frustration spilled onto her arm, almost putting out her cigarette. She wouldn't be such a prctty girl any more. God knows what the years had done to her. Maybe a Valium, she thought, or a Lude. Then she was looking down into the angry eyes of her eight-year-old adopted daughter Jessica Jorrish, who was smiling cross-eyed at her. The child was up to something. When they had adopted her, selecting carefully from the rest of the blond-haired, blue-eyed babies, she had been quite sure she and Tom had made the right choice. But their luck had gone awry when they lost Mr. Chips.

Almost drained of energy, Rachael picked up the paper, determined Tom wouldn't find it. As she headed for the wastebasket in the kitchen she saw what the overweight little girl with the stringy dishwater hair had done. A box of crayons spilled all over the floor but the priceless wallpaper had been used as a coloring book.

"Jessica!" she screeched and saw the little girl's wispy, revengeful smile. She felt like spanking her but she didn't know how to start now. They had never disciplined the child, only given her things.

Stuffing the paper into the wastebasket, she rushed up the steps crying, heading for that room. Cautiously, she turned the door handle and peeked in. The powder-blue room was the same as it had been ten years ago. Only the maid came in to dust the crib and the little rocking chair and the picture, the only picture of little Joshua, the one with the wind blowing his fair hair and the smile reflecting one dear little baby tooth. Tiptoeing softly as if the baby was napping, she went to the edge of the pillow and kissed it, pretending his silky little head was resting on it as it had ten years ago.

Downstairs Jessica had finger-walked her box of crayons toward the kitchen. Someday she would be a famous designer, so she had to redo everything. Then she spotted the open newspaper in the wastebasket and spread it out on the floor. No good, it looked like it was waiting for dog poopie. She would have to decorate it. She would color a picture for her daddy. Tongue sticking out of the side of her mouth, she decided on green. That was a nice color and it was the color of money so Daddy should like that a lot. Then she would leave her present where Daddy would be sure to find it. He loved to read his paper when he got home from the office.

SHE loved the new feeling of having so much to do for herself and racing through the day to get it all done. She made sure her machine was on and then ran over to the big supermarket on the highway to pick up some groceries. After that she might print more fliers. She had found the stationery store that would Xerox for her. Tomorrow she would go to the paper and put a small classified ad in it. She dumped her groceries on the kitchen table. All the ads on TV in the slammer featured mouth-watering things they would never get to eat.

Cornflakes, steak, salad dressing, fresh vegetables, ice cream. Ice cream. She hadn't had ice cream in ten years.

Something else was in the room. Then she saw the little red button. It was flashing on and off like a neon sign, like a warning. She heard it go through the frightening banging noises until someone said: "This is a message for Gourmet-to-Go. My son gave me your little flier. I have a small party I'll need done, something special. Call Mrs. Edwards at 958-0965. God, nothing personal, but I hate talking into these machines."

B.J. smiled. She would have to make a note of that, that Mrs. Edwards hates the machine. Well, she did too.

B.J. smiled. Then without any warning, the machine skipped on to another message: "Saw your flier on a telephone pole. What a coincidence. I have a child's birthday party party coming up and I'm having a baby. My name is Ann Richards. I'm at 675-8977."

B.J. stared at the damn thing in amazement. She couldn't believe it. Her first day and she had two jobs. She was going to make it. She took out the vanilla/chocolate swirl ice cream. It was a save-for-later but this was different. She had something to celebrate and she ate it out of the carton with a big spoon.

Then she rewound the messages so she could double-check if she had gotten everything. It was playing her message as well. Shaking, she pressed the silver bar again and heard the frightened voice that was hers: "Hi, this is Gourmet-to-Go. We're not in right now but if you leave your name and number at the sound of the beep, we'll get back to you.''

The "we" was a little optimistic. But no one would ever know who was talking.

HE stood in the shadows of the drooping tree by the slimy water and waited. It was night. He loved the night. It had been about ten years ago when he had waited in the stormy rain for exactly the right moment.

The house up on the hill wasn't lavender anymore. The paint had peeled and tall weeds circled the house. Once the lawn had resembled a miniature golf course. The rich people had rented the house out for a few years after the thing happened, but now it just sat there. It would be torn down soon for a row of plastic look-alike houses.

Madison wasn't a summer resort anymore. The garbage had floated around too long in Lake Erie. He laughed to himself. No one could take the garbage out.

Sometimes he liked to come here by the ravine, all alone under the night stars, and relive that powerful night when he had changed everybody's life. Then squeezing hard on his best friend, whispering softly to himself, he would aim high so the juice shot into the sky. It was the best. For no one ever knew what he did or what he had done that magical night.

He looked up at the house that would be no more.

She knew.

And they had let her out. This time he would have to be more careful about how and when he killed her.

# Chapter Fifteen

WEARING a royal-blue skirt with thin white ruffle on the bottom and a white T-shirt top, she grabbed the keys to the van and rushed out. Leroy waved to her and she smiled. Why was he always outside when she was?

If the girls in prison could see her now. She hadn't felt this elation since Fat Florence was found facedown in her cell hugging her knife. She had shut out all the house sounds and slept last night on the top of the bed and she felt terrific. No one would ever hurt her again.

Peering through the window, she found it. A storefront with black and white awnings that said *The Salem Voice*. She parked the van right on Main Street and walked through the big glass doors.

A young woman who had been typing turned somewhat around, surprised to find anyone standing there.

"I'd, uh, like to place a classified ad," B.J. said.

"Oh, sure." The young woman handed her a pencil. "Twenty-five characters to the line, five dollars, minimum four lines."

B.J. took out the ad she had written. It would never fit. Twirling a piece of her newly blond hair, which she didn't ever think she'd get used to, she bent over the jigsaw puzzle of words. She didn't notice a tall, thin,

146

unbelievably attractive man with black curly hair and glass-blue eyes looking down humorously at her.

"Stuck?" he said.

She looked up, startled.

"Let's see what you have."

As he looked over her scrawny handwriting, B.J. resented him, whoever he was. Finally he pointed at the piece of paper. "You need to put 'prices reasonable' or something like that. Tell you what. I'll give you ten extra words free as a good-luck gift. New in town?"

"Are you sure your boss won't mind?" she said.

He grinned at her. "I'll ask him later. But I think not. Have time for a quick cup of coffee?"

B.J. shook her head and said softly, "No thanks, I can't." She watched him walk away and could never remember having felt that way. He was probably the best-looking man she had ever seen. She hadn't really answered his question because she had been afraid to.

The typist giggled. "That *was* the boss. How many weeks?" She reached inside her envelope and took out enough money for the ad to run two weeks. Her phone number was in the ad but not her name.

The woman took a receipt book. "Your name?"

She stumbled at first. She couldn't remember that name. "Barbara Marshall." Red-faced, she gave her address. He was standing at a desk close by. She could feel it. When she snapped around, she saw he was looking at her. He walked a little closer.

"You must be the new girl in town. I thought they'd never unload that place. You rented the Haunted House?" He was grinning mischievously and suddenly B.J. saw that his face was terribly lined for someone so young and handsome. He had smile lines, eye lines, forehead lines. "We did a piece on that once."

B.J. smiled weakly but said nothing. With his eyes on her, as if he wanted to say something else, he watched her walk out. She didn't know who this man

147

was, she didn't like men who looked like that, but she had never walked feeling like every joint was disconnected and her knees would cave in any second.

AFTER parking the van, she walked slowly to the supermarket, grabbing a cart. She wondered why rejecting a handsome stranger who asked her for a cup of coffee was causing her to obsess like this.

She reached for the cake flour. Maybe he just wanted to welcome her to town. Honey for the carrot cake and sugar for the big birthday sheet cake. Of course, a man like that would have to be married. Gum drops or the M&M's for the birthday cake? Undecided, she snatched both. Maybe she was afraid of men. Maybe that was it. The only men she had known were prison guards; the boys from Madison had been boys. Black, curly hair. No, she didn't like it. The lightning had framed the man's face that night the baby was killed.

In Aisle 4 she stopped and had an all-too-familiar pep talk with herself. Now, this has to stop. She remembered Bubbles's gift of the two thousand dollars and also the condition. Forget about your revenge. If she didn't work hard it would dwindle, and then where would she be? She wouldn't have even enough money for the groceries. Keep your mind on your goals, she told herself, taking a few packages of food coloring. By the time she reached Aisle 5 she was debating on which brand of chicken to buy for the chicken salad. As she lugged her chart to the checkout counter it was groaning with enough groceries for two parties and people were looking at her. Standing in line, she thumbed through an article about the marriage of a one-hundred-year-old man to a fourteen-year-old girl and then put it down, unsatisfied. But she had completely forgotten about the man who had flirted with her.

Through the rest of the afternoon, throughout a brief thundershower, even while mopping up after she accidentally broke two eggs on the floor, she kept singing and working.

"Hey, you have a nice voice."

She looked and jumped back, reaching for the mop. "How long have you been standing there?"

"Oh, the doorbell doesn't work and I knocked but you didn't hear me. Can I come in?"

"You are in," B.J. said. "I don't want to be rude, but I'm in an awful rush and . . . was something wrong with my ad?"

Joe Peterson stood in the hot, fragrant kitchen and looked around the house. One of the most beautiful women he had ever seen had walked into his paper today and he was enough of a reporter to try to meet her.

"I came to buy a carrot cake," he said, smiling sheepishly.

"Oh?" she said. *Was that all?*

"Keep working. I'll just sit down for a while. Taking a little break."

She found it hard to work with him watching her. *What is he really after?*

He sat and drummed his fingers on the table, watching her back. Maybe he shouldn't have come. *Now how was he going to ask her out?*

"I'll have to bake the carrot cake with the rest of the batch," she said, placing the chicken in a pot.

He began to feel very uncomfortable, as if he just wanted to run out of the door. But it was his first attraction since . . .

"Would you like a cup of coffee?" she asked stiffly. She felt like adding "while you're waiting," but she didn't know what he was waiting for. She glanced over and saw him nodding.

"How come a gorgeous girl like yourself isn't married?"

149

Bad opening but at least he had cut the spooky silence.

She turned around to the black curly hair just appearing suddenly in her new life. It scared her. She felt like saying that no one bothered to get married in prison but washed her hands and ended up with "Oh, I don't know. And you? How come you never married?"

"Well, I did," he said, as she brought him a coffee mug, a creamer, and sugar.

The mug almost slipped out of her hands but she grabbed it. So he had a wife but he liked to play around? What was she doing with this strange man in her kitchen?

"I mean, she died. She and my baby son were killed in an automobile accident. You know the most terrible part?" he said passionately. "My son wasn't even two years old."

She didn't know what to do or say. Finally, the first thing that came into her head. "I'm sorry." Quickly she went over and turned the oven back on, thinking he wouldn't want to know she had been locked in a jail because everyone thought she killed a baby almost the same age.

"Turn around," he said and as she turned around a flash went off.

"Hey," she said, hands on her hips. "I don't like to have my picture taken."

He put the camera down immediately. "I'm sorry. Most people are flattered. This is a new camera I'm trying out. You should be very photogenic." He was staring at the kitchen counter. "Oh, I would use the M&M's," he said.

"I thought the gumdrops."

"Oh no, the M&M's get all gooey and melt all over their faces. Much more fun." He stood up to leave. "My wife used to do a little catering . . ."

He looked down at her. It still hurt to talk about his wife, dammit. He didn't know how to do this. Ask a

150

beautiful young woman out for a date? How long had it been—three years now?

Especially with someone who wasn't even interested. Who couldn't care less if he disappeared.

"Maybe we could run a spread. We often do that on small businesses. Call it 'Takin' Care of Business,' and we give you a boost with some free ad space. Also we give you a poster to put in your window."

She felt a moment of panic. That would be all she needed. She shook her head no. "It's not necessary, Mr. Peterson, really."

He held out his hand and smiled.

It was a beautiful smile. She wished he would leave. *I don't know how to do this,* she thought. Finally she laughed and said, "It's even smaller than a small business. And if I take more orders I'll have to hire someone, and I'm not ready for that."

She had a beautiful laugh. They stood looking at each other and then a bell went off. B.J. almost jumped. "The timer," she explained and pulled her hand out of the warmth of his.

"I'm sorry," she said, flushed.

"That's okay, Barbara." He knew her name and address. The classified ad.

His hand was on the screen door. Again that impish, boyish smile in the sad face. "I'll be back."

She looked up at him but she couldn't smile back.

"To pick up my carrot cake," he said and closed the screen door behind him.

THE Rapid Transit pulled into the Shaker Heights station right on the dot. Tom Jorrish folded his *Wall Street Journal* under his right arm and carried his heavy brown briefcase in his left one. Rachael's blue Honda wasn't there. He waited five minutes and then decided this was going to be one of those days. Come to think of it, Rachael hadn't been acting like herself lately. Then,

151

too, there were so many places she had to take Jessica to—her ballet class or her art class or to the child psychiatrist they finally found for her. Best in Cleveland. Charged enough money.

Trooping stoically to the nearby bus stop, his shoes kicking up dust, he thought, as he did many times, of his adopted daughter. They had decided on a girl and he had had visions of this pretty little thing in frilly dresses, entwining her arms around his neck, cooing, "Daddy."

Instead of the luck factor, they had lucked out. She had never been anything but a constant headache. But then, it was their fault. You could never be sure about an adopted child. About what was really in the genes.

Now, Joshie would have been different. There was a perfect little boy, bright as a penny, even as a little baby. Joshua. Little Josh. That's all he had ever been, a baby. Sitting on the bus, crumpling the edges of his paper. After all these years, after all the sessions with Dr. Trumbell, he knew he shouldn't be thinking about it. He knew all that. But he was being a little bit bad today. He needed a drink, that's all.

By the time he was climbing up his long cobblestone path, wondering why the gardener hadn't pulled the weeds a little better this summer, he knew he had managed to shake his unwelcome obsession.

Unlocking the heavy door, he stepped inside his house.

"Rachael?" he shouted. "Rachael? I'm home."

But no one answered him back. The house was cool and still.

Tom sighed. There were two things he liked at the end of a hard day at the office. To be kissed hello by his wife and to sit back in his black, leather recliner and sip a dry martini. He went to the bar. Well, at least, he could have one.

It was on the top of the bar. At first he was going to

crumple it up as garbage and toss it. It was a newspaper he couldn't get in the office and read at home, *The Cleveland Plain Dealer*. But this was scribbled up and almost unreadable. God, but Jessica irritated him sometimes. Art lessons, indeed.

Just before the paper slid off the marble bartop he noticed a small headline underneath the crayon drawings. He put down his drink and when he had finished deciphering it, the paper was on the floor and he was pacing the room nervously.

She was free.

That tricky girl had been unleashed on society to do what? To kill another innocent baby? She was out on the streets after only ten years. It was a mistake. They should have sent her to the gas chamber.

He replayed the picture in his mind, the heartbreaking tale of Rachael talking and cooing to the dead baby. Soothing it, stroking it, as if it were still alive. *It.* That's what you call a dead baby. Quickly he bunched up the newspaper, took it outside into the garden, reached for his lighter, and set it a flame.

Rachael must never know.

There was no telling what she might do.

# Chapter Sixteen

IT was ten the next morning and B.J.'s hands were shaking. Carefully she topped the cakes and platters with Saran Wrap. Oh God, what if they didn't like it? The birthday party was her first delivery. She carried everything out, almost reverently, to the van, eyed the sky, and prayed it wouldn't rain. Birthday parties needed sunshine.

Bending over the wheel, as if she were driving in a blizzard, she searched for the address. It was the first house on the hill, though Athens was full of hills and curves, like a city from another century. The leaves were just beginning to get a rusty cast and drop from the trees that lined the outlying streets of the college town.

The carrot cake for him was baked and put aside. Would be come back? Maybe he would be busy or forget. But it was there. She found the right address. What was she doing thinking about Joe Peterson at a time like this?

She began unloading the car, noticing that tremor in her hands, and she wondered if anyone could see. "These are the little potato puffs and they taste just like French fries," B.J. told the young mother. "And these are tiny, little hot dogs rolled in cheese, wrapped in bacon, with the hot dog rolls baked around them. You just have to heat them up. Here's the carrot and raisin slaw and here's cheeseburger pie, something I made up. Oh, and do you have ice cream? And here's the cake.'' Everyone looked down at the huge orange cake with the white-and-blue icing drawing of a baseball catcher.

"That's real nice," the woman said, looking like she was going to have the baby any second.

"Are you from Athens?" another woman said and was introduced as a sister-in-law, while another was the mother-in-law. They stared at her as she continued to check down through her notebook, noting the date to come back and collect the pans and trays she made everything in.

"Oh, Northern Ohio," she said, watching the mother writing out a check. It would be her first paycheck and for a second she felt thrilled and very proud of herself.

"Why did you settle in these parts?" the mother-in-law persisted.

"Oh," B.J. said, stuck for an answer, just wanting to get the check and go. "Well, my mother and her people were from around here, you know."

"Because you look kind of familiar," the mother-in-law said. "Doesn't she?"

Her daughter nodded.

B.J. looked at the door.

"Maybe that television actress on that new series with all the dogs," said the mother-in-law.

"Naw," said the daughter. The pregnant mother handed her a check with a smile and B.J. almost backed out the door. Would they realize later who she was? Did they even know? If the word got out that an ex-con was catering children's birthday parties, somebody else would get the job.

* * *

THE red signal on her machine was blinking, when she finally came in the door, bringing the platters that she had taken from this job. She let the screen door slam behind her and then got a piece of paper and a pencil to take down yet another order: "This is you-know-who. When you can get away, come over and let's have another little drink. Oh, yes, it's Leroy. Remember him?"

Then there were all those beep and rattle sounds and then the machine shut off and no little lights were flashing. She stared at the machine and shook her head. A nosy neighbor—after she had taken such great pains to protect herself. There was something about him she didn't like. She didn't want to get too close to anybody right now. It was too dangerous.

JOE Peterson took a bottle of Johnnie Walker Red from his file cabinets. It had been filed under S.

"So whaddya think?" Joe asked his friend eagerly.

The man on the other side of the desk, Irwin Norris, sat playing with his checkered felt hat and took a glass of scotch. "This is it?" Norris asked.

Before he could reply to Norris's question, which would only be an insulted response, Joe said, "You want me to come back to the *Post*, with manufactured news? No, I'm staying with my own paper. I'm going to build it into the best voice in Southern Ohio, even the Midwest. Stephanie knew I wanted to do this. I used her insurance money. I have to make a go of it here. Here I can write what I want to. It's my paper."

Irwin nodded solemnly, picking up a typed draft, a small column about a cat stuck in a tree, who brought out enough troops for a four-alarm fire. "Is this your idea of a really hot story?" he said, holding up the cat-in-tree copy. "There *are* no stories in this one-horse town. Come to your senses, sell the paper to some sucker, and come back to New York, where you belong." Then he said almost as a begrudging after-thought, "They'll almost double your pay."

Joe turned his back on his old friend from New York and answered with "We got one lettuce and four beautiful tomatoes. Delicious. Ever walk into your own garden with a salt shaker?"

"Aren't you going to ask me any questions? Like what's the pay exactly? Most reporters would be a little curious. And don't you want to talk about your by-line?"

Joe turned slowly around and took some paper clips out from inside his jacket. "Irwin, tomorrow if World War III should suddenly begin, the *New York Post* would be more concerned about movie stars and celebrities. *Ax Killer Snuffs Beautiful Blond.* And that's news?

"It's just a 'bright' and you know it. I thought you flew out for a day of fishing and country living, to be where everything's green. Why this lecture?"

Irwin nodded and then said, "It's just that a few of us were worried when, after the funeral, you just took off that way. Now I know it must have been terrible to wake up one day and poof everything's gone, but why this when you have such a great future with the *Post?*"

On Joe's desk there was a picture of his son, Scottie, wearing powder-blue short pants with straps and a white blouse. He had blond curly hair, just like Stephanie's, and his bright blue eyes teased the camera. A beautiful little boy, he was hugging his Teddy bear.

"So, what do you do for fun around here?" Norris said, realizing it was an untactful way to switch the conversation, after he had said it.

"Same thing you do," Joe said and his former colleague heard the hurt and insult in his voice. "I work. There's a gin mill around the corner. Mostly men from the factory who watch the games and play a little pinball. I fish. I have my garden out back." "Out back,"

Irwin Norris recorded with his reporter's mind. There *was* no "out back" in New York City. "There's a good library and some drive-ins. Toward Athens there's some lovely restaurants and some bars and nearer to Columbus there's—"

Irwin Norris held out his hands like a stop signal, as if he couldn't take anymore.

"And I suppose you've started on the Great American Novel."

"Maybe," Joe said.

Irwin picked up a copy of the latest weekly edition of the *Salem Voice* lying on Joe's desk. He opened it up to a full-page ad from a hardware store.

The centerfold section contained the classified ads. Irwin put the paper down. "So I can't persuade you to come back to work for us again? You're happy?"

Joe looked at his old friend and drinking buddy, who was now dripping cigar ashes on a hooked rug Joe had picked up at a flea market one day. Joe wanted to counter with "Who's happy?" Irwin had found his desk interesting reading and he found the glossies he had taken of Barbara Marshall.

"Your next story?"

"Dark room back of the other room," Joe said. "No, just a woman I met. Does catering. I was testing out a new camera. She ran a classified ad in the paper. Doesn't want to take up any more space than that. I bought a carrot cake from her."

"Goddammit, you sly son of a bitch. She's gorgeous. So you're having some fun after all. I was beginning to wonder."

Joe laughed and came around and clapped his old buddy on the back. "C'mon, let me drive you to the airport."

But Irwin was still staring at the photographs. He picked up one and then another. "You know, she looks familiar," he said at last. "Can't place it but I know I've seen the face before."

Joe stood up thinking of all the times Irwin had to have the last answer. "She's just very beautiful and she's from Ohio."

Irwin stood up. Joe was probably right, but he had been a reporter for a long time, sometimes too long.

No, the face was familiar. He just couldn't place it.

His old buddy had been deposited in the Athens airport long before, and Joe sat in his office. The newspaper had been put to bed for the night and it was dark except for the one light in his office. As he often did when he was alone, he liked to talk to the picture of his dead son as if he had gotten a chance to grow up.

"Do you think I made a mistake, Scottie? Your old man was a hot reporter and now look at me, in a dinky one-horse town with a twelve-page newspaper to run."

He leaned back in his swivel chair and the photograph said nothing. "But it was ten pages when I bought it." Some noise interrupted. He looked around. It was no one. Just the sounds of Salem, Ohio, on a summer night.

Slowly he walked back down to his little office and picked up his paper, smiling proudly. Classified ads were growing. Two pages now. With his finger he traced the column under Services, but couldn't find her ad. Had they left it out? Then he realized it was too soon. The next paper.

He walked out of the office again and found the Roladex file where he had gotten her address and her name. What he needed now was her phone number. Too bad they had finished the scotch. It hadn't been the best day of his life.

And then there was B.J. He hadn't been attracted to a woman quite that way since Steph.

"Think your mom would mind, Scottie-boy?" he asked the photograph, walking back into his office. "Sometimes your dad gets awfully lonely."

Without giving himself a chance to back out, he dialed the number and as soon as he heard the first hi, he began to speak but he realized she was out, too.

"Hi, this is Gourmet-to-Go. We're not in right now but if you leave your name and number at the sound of the beep, we'll get back to you."

He held the receiver for one second then watched it clatter down on the phone. Sighing, he stood up and headed down the street to the tavern. Maybe it was better she didn't pick up. Who needed a rejection on a bad day?


"MAGAZINE?"

Irwin Norris stared at her pretty feet and took his eyes all the way past her nylon-sheathed legs all the way up to her frown. He accepted a magazine and fastened his seat belt. Damned glad to go back to New York. There was something about Ohio, about small towns anywhere, that depressed him.

Pushing his seat back, he remembered the old days when Stephanie was alive. Now, there was a love match. Until that phone call that had come to him first, because Joe was out covering a story. He had felt like it was *his* wife and kid who had been killed by some nut with a driver's license he didn't know how to use.

He could remember the phone call and what happened after that like it was yesterday. That's one of the things that made him a great—maybe jaded—but great reporter. He had always had that ability to remember. He could see whole images, like movies playing in his mind. What color tie the president had worn at an inauguration, what kind of hat his wife had worn, how many clouds in the sky.

It didn't make sense that his memory could fail him now. He pounded his fist on the arm of the chair and the woman next to him looked at him thoughtfully before looking away.

# Chapter Seventeen

SHE liked to work early in the morning and she loved the sunshine that lit up her kitchen and filled it with love. There hadn't been much of it in her life. Again she found herself thinking about Joe Peterson; she had never felt such an attraction for a man. Nor so frightened by it. She didn't think it possible. The timer went off and she took the cakes out and set them to cool. She had baked an extra cake. It was in the refrigerator wrapped in plastic and tied with a pumpkin-colored ribbon.

She was so lost in thought that it wasn't until seconds later that she realized someone was knocking at the door.

Thinking it could only be Leroy so early in the morning, she was shocked when she opened the screen door.

"I came to buy my carrot cake," Joe said, stepping cautiously into the fragrant kitchen. "And to give you these." He handed her a small pile of the 8 × 10 glossies he had taken of her.

B.J. looked at the shots. Like all the other pictures she had seen of herself but with light blond hair. As she put them on the table to get the carrot cake, he said, "Listen, I have to apologize for the other day. I'm a little rusty and maybe I came on too strong. Is that it? Or is there someone else?"

She shook her head, putting the cake down. "No, there's no one."

"Then let me take you out to dinner tonight, nothing more, just a nice quiet dinner."

"It's just that I have a lot of work to do," she said, finally not knowing what to do, desperately wanting someone else in the room. Why had she picked that name? Everybody was named Barbara.

"It's only dinner. Please. I feel lonely." She looked up into his deep, blue eyes staring into hers, his gray pull-over sweater and his curly black hair, and she found herself saying yes. She had known instinctively what age-old buttons someone else could punch.

"Pick you up at seven, okay?" He wanted to get out of there before she changed her mind.

Promising herself she would have dinner with him just this once, she turned back to the kitchen and tried to figure out just where she was.

THERE was a half-eaten doughnut and a container of muddy coffee on his desk. It was almost martini time. The offices on South Street, home of the *New York Post*, sounded the same as usual, one steady buzz. What Irwin Norris should have been doing that late morning was using his two-fingered typing style to write a front-page story about a murdered coed found in the wilds of New Jersey.

But strangely, he wasn't doing that.

Not three, but four in the morning he had awoken in his sprawling West Side apartment with a throbbing headache. He had remembered. If he was right—and he usually was—his old buddy had a shock wave coming his way.

When he got into work he made sure he got all the files on that old case; they went all the way back to

1978. They covered the sensational trial in Cleveland, Ohio, but it was the latest clipping that had jarred his memory.

*Beautiful Baby-Killer Granted Parole After Ten Years.*

In the picture, the hair was a little darker but what the hell. How much was a bottle of hair dye?

The headline was almost as long as the article. He fingered it. Maybe the broad was what was keeping him there. If he told Joe the truth, there was a good chance he would come back.

His hand reached for the phone. All around him there was activity, phones ringing, shouting, typewriters and televisions going, computers printing out. He remembered what Joe said: "I didn't ever think my life would be material for the *New York Post.*" That's all the fucker said when he went with him to view the almost unidentifiably mangled bodies. He couldn't let him get hurt again.

But one second before he picked up the phone it rang. There was another murder in that wooded section of that place in New Jersey. He stopped only to put on his jacket, brushing the clippings to the side.

He didn't know which was worse—to tell the guy or let him find out for himself. Poor Joe. He just didn't have any luck with women. Coward that he was, he let his secretary call him and read the article.

WHEN she noticed he had left the carrot cake on the table, she immediately ran out the screen door, squinting in the sunshine, wondering if he had left.

"Joe!"

He was just getting into his car, hoping like hell she hadn't decided to back out. She was running, almost stumbling in the grass. He couldn't help but smile. Just in that moment, in the late summer sunshine, she reminded him of a teenager.

"You forgot your cake."

"What do I owe you?"

She stared at him for a second then said, "Aw, forget it."

"Okay. I'll buy you a drink tonight, how's that?"

She nodded. If he did that, it would be her second drink in her life. When she came back into the kitchen, she remembered a reason why she couldn't go out to dinner with him.

She had nothing to wear.

She couldn't wear pants and a top, and she couldn't spare the time or the money to buy a dress. Maybe a white blouse to go over the dark royal-blue skirt with the inch of ruffle at the bottom.

When she returned with a frilly blouse with puffy sleeves, she still wasn't sure she had gotten the right thing. At five to seven she was putting on the lipstick she had gotten in prison, an inch-size tube of light coral. At one minute to seven, pacing around the kitchen she heard a knock on the door. The doorbell was dead. She'd have to call the landlady about that soon.

Joe came in wearing a navy sports jacket and a bright red tie. "You know, I'm almost afraid to take you out to dinner. You probably cook better than anybody else. But I know a beautiful little country inn not far from here, where we can eat in the garden."

They were walking out to the car when he said, "You know, you should keep that screen door locked. It's not safe."

"Oh, that little thing is broken," she said. "I usually keep the kitchen door locked shut except when it gets too hot."

Her next-door neighbor was sitting at the little white table on his open patio. She waved to him and noticed that he pointedly didn't wave back.

\* \* \*

165

SHIPLEY'S Inn was set back from the road, hidden by a row of weeping willows. To get to the garden restaurant in the back, you walked through the hotel and the ancient desk clerk pointed the way. B.J. looked around the garden setting and thought this was everything she had dreamed about during the long years staring at bars. Joe ordered two frothy drinks with exotic names and after the first sips, she felt tingly, warned herself not to get too high.

"Tell me about yourself," Joe said, looking into her eyes.

She looked away.

"Shy?"

"Oh, I just don't like to be in the spotlight, that's all," she said, eyes to the side, making it up as she went along. Something that sounded not too fake, not too ordinary. "I had a job in—Cleveland, just a secretary. And when they went out of business I decided to strike out on my own. I always wanted to be a caterer." She swallowed.

"Well, where did you learn to bake? I nibbled on that carrot cake and it was great, just great, you know? Where did you learn to do that?"

She smiled. "Well, that's what mothers are for," she said.

The waitress came up and they both ordered the chicken pot pie, a specialty. She looked at the men in jackets and the women in pretty dresses and thought, for a minute, that they were all looking at her, that they all knew who she was.

Joe seemed to field any questions about himself, wanting to know more about her. Why did he want to know so much?

They drove home, the sky between twilight and deep night, and he told her all his amusing anecdotes about running a paper in a small town. As he parked in the car in the yard, he leaned forward. For a split second she thought he might kiss her, but no, he reached across and opened her door. Under the purple-pink sky, she could see him smiling up at her.

"I'll call you. Let's do it again sometime."

When she let herself in, she waltzed around the kitchen happily, holding the edges of her ruffled skirt. It was a minute or two before she noticed her flashing answering machine. More orders. This was amazing. More than she had hoped for. She grabbed her pad and a pen and sat on the top of the table reaching over to punch the silver bar, still thinking about sitting in the open-air garden, having dinner. She waited for the order, smiling.

"Hi, I'm calling Gourmet-to-Go. To tell you that I'm going to kill you, B.J. Stronger, when you least expect it. Just like you killed that baby. You don't have a chance. Soon, you'll be dead."

The pen fell out of her hands and she heard it rolling across the floor. That voice, raspy and hoarse. Disguised somehow. But it knew who she was, where she was. She jumped up and put her finger on the button to shut it off, but then she pulled it off frantically when she realized the machine was still going: "Your days are numbered, B.J. Stronger. When you least expect it you're going to die. Pray for yourself, B.J. No one else can."

Trapped, she clutched on to the table, her breathing coming in deep gasps, as she shook her head, a prisoner, waiting for more. When the machine beeped, she screamed so long that she had to put her hands on her ears not to hear. Then there was calm. Silence in the house. Except for the sounds in a house: the refrigerator's hum, a fly buzzing overhead.

She slid on a little bit of margarine that had fallen on the floor and crashed into the cabinet where her fingers found what she wanted. Clutching it desperately, she rushed to the front door to double-check that it was locked. Then she ran to all the windows and slammed them shut.

Whimpering, she put her chair smack in front of the table, facing the door, the knife held out in front of her. The latch on the screen door—it was broken! How could she have been so stupid. Scrambling so fast, her sandals half on, she tripped, slamming and locking the door so that the dishes in the sink rattled. She looked around the little house, at the ugly machine, and knew she was locked inside an airless tomb. Shaking, shivering, knowing she could call no one. Not even the police because they would know who she was and then no one would believe her and the killer would kill her before they came.

She sat down, her huge knife aimed like a weapon, and reached under the little table where the phone was. She pulled the plug out of the answering machine and sat holding it, sobbing jaggedly, waiting for . . . what?

There wasn't a sound except for a dog barking somewhere. Then she looked up at the ceiling and suddenly remembered. She never had figured out why the floorboards creaked upstairs.

# Chapter Eighteen

IT was quiet in the house. She turned on the lights. She was safe only if the lights were out. She picked up a long butcher knife. Her only companion. But she couldn't leave from this space.

Even if there was a fire engine going by she would not move. Not a muscle. She would listen to the sounds of her apartment. Nothing was coming from overhead. The doors were sealed shut.

It was so stuffy and quiet in her prison cell. Except for a fly.

"Little fly? Little fly? What were you in another life?" Damn fly. Everything was stuck in space. Everything was stuck. Everything. Thing. All the minute things in her life, she looked at with new importance. Click. Her days might be numbered. Click. Very numbered. Numbered. Numb. Waiting for the killer. Waiting to be killed.

IT was close to closing time when the boss looked over his sales team and then looked in the yard. He saw something in the plate of glass that made him angry.

"You men just turned into a lot of pencil shovers and paper pushers." One of the men got up and put on his jacket. "Man out there. I'll go."

"Sorry, Sonny, I spotted him first. No, I'll leave you eager beavers here to figure out your commissions and I'll go outside and show you how to sell."

He walked directly over to the handsome stranger, who was carrying his jacket slung over his shoulder. He put on his felt hat and the tall, thin salesman pumped his arm. "Hi, I own the joint but I'm coming out to practice my selling."

He warmed right away into his pitch. "Looking at this silver 1986 Impala, well, that's a brilliant choice. That's the car. I swear this car was driven by a little old lady who's finally going into a nursing home. It is God's truth, I'll tell you, that she used this car only twice a week. On Wednesday for her grocery shopping and on Sunday morning for church."

He was rocking back and forth now, warming to the sound of his own voice. "Or," he paused, "is there another car you want?" Cold fish, he thought to himself.

"No, I'd like to think this over." He pulled out his notebook.

"Didn't hear your name, young fella. I'm Wilton Stronger, owner of the lot—lock, stock, and barrel, and all the tired salesmen. You got the best, kiddo, tell me what you want."

"Actually some information, if I can."

"Cops? I thought we were done with that." He looked at the stranger with a new glance.

He shook hands with the owner. "I'm Joe Peterson. And I've come all the way to Madison to talk to you about a book I'm supposed to write.

*Guilty Until Proven Innocent.* It's about famous trials where they resembled a witch-hunt."

"Won't sell. Why don't you guys ever write one of them sexy thrillers? Now, that sells. One thing I can't stand is an intellectual. Wouldn't give a buck fifty for famous trials. Not unless there was sex in it, like I says.

Damn if you boys get me all the time. And I do mean *all* the time. Not another word. I've given enough. Okay, I'll give you four minutes and the fifth minute I'll fart.''

"I didn't say I wasn't interested in buying a car. But, truthfully, I'd like some information. If we can exonerate your sister, she would be free. Do you think she had a fair trial?''

"Yessir, I think she did. That lawyer fellar was good for her. Yassir, Mr. Peterson, B.J. was—is still, I think—a wee bit crazy, doesn't come down enough for us poor mortals. She's nutsy. But then again, no one takes her seriously. She's just B.J. God gave her beauty but not brains. Ya see what I mean?''

"Do you think she killed that baby?''

"Listen, save yourself some time and me too. I'm all tuckered out. Give me a manure or two and I'll find you a better car.''

"So you think she's guilty on all counts?''

"Mister, is the Pope a Catholic?''

"But at the trial, you said she wasn't.'' Wilton tried to recollect ten years ago and pulled a piece of long weed growing through the sides of the lot and swished it around like a long, green toothpick.

"You have anything to do with her?''

"Nothing. Hear she's living right near Mentor.''

The reporter said nothing.

"Now, I'm going to ask you off my lot. That's enough info for today. You people are born pests. You want to know what I think? I'm not one of those liberal people. I think she's guilty because that's what happened at the trial. They don't make no real good mistakes like that. And B.J., well, the opinion was she buzzed out. Now there's a car over there might suit you.

"How'd you like a job with me? Pays pretty good. You're persistent, I'll give you that but I'll say that you better get off my lot.'' Then the voice he was trying to cover up showed through. "Or else, mister, I'll throw you out. And at night, we have the dogs to keep you company."

"One more thing," Peterson said, walking to the office, having to run to keep up with him. "She's not in Mentor. She's in Athens, Ohio, right near Columbus and she has a catering business called Gourmet-to-Go."

"Not one more thing," the owner of the lot said. He slammed the door behind him, and turned off all the lights on the lot.

SHE was tired but the terror wouldn't let her rest. Everything was in its place and locked. Every door and window and whatever else she could find to zip up. She could hear herself breathing. Sharp, jagged breaths. She wondered where people were.

Her grandparents were dead. Willie was where he was. Never moved. Hometown boy. She never wanted to see him again. This Joe, she would rather call him "Joey," he was hard at work in his paper. It was a nice little paper. As papers go. Maybe he said that about the food she catered. Nice little jobs as jobs go. But she loved it. She wasn't exactly doing it now.

Everything was in its place. But her life. That had stopped.

HE crossed the dirt road and went into the Damian Diner. It was ostensibly to have "Coffee and . . ."

It was about six, a little after, when he, dog tired, needed a perk. "Coffee and what are those little things?"

"Sweet rolls, have one?" The waitress smiled at him.

"Say, do you know when that used car lot opened?"

She shrugged. "Before my time, you know? Wait up. Say, Jo-Bob, you remember when that lot of Wilton's opened up?"

The short-order cook and obvious owner said, "Yes,

I do. It's damn near the tenth anniversary. Yep, ten years almost today."

"Works out great for us," she said. "We get his customers and they take a breather here and then they go back. We'll be working on a commission soon." She laughed.

Joe Peterson wiped his napkin on his lip. He was hoping for more but then again he was grasping at straws. This was going to be all he'd get. This time.

THE upstairs was going strong. Well, she couldn't live with that. She'd go upstairs. It was probably the bat. She took a knife and ran up the steps, brandishing her knife like a pirate.

The door was open, noisy in the wind, but nevertheless open. She went in and gingerly picked up the lamp that was rolling back and forth in the wind. The shutter should come off.

Carefully she left, creeping down the steps midway. Until she stopped, not knowing where to go as she heard her downstairs door slam shut.

THE reporter went through his notebook. "Do you know a Debbie Newsom?"

"Oh, no." The waitress laughed and poured some more coffee in his cup. "She's Debbie Turk now."

"No kidding, she married Frankie? Huh, never would have thought it."

He was getting strange looks from the waitress. "Selling yearbooks?" she finally asked.

"No, I'm a reporter from New York."

"More articles about the sister, what's her name?"

"B.J. Stronger," he said.

"Yeah, I had a big surprise. You wouldn't have believed her to be a killer. Just a lot of silliness on her part. We don't think that young girl committed that awful crime? Do we, Jo-Bob?" He shrugged. "Family disowned her. Must be mighty lonely. I mean who did she make friends with in prison? Real tragedy that case. Who would have thought it.''

"You."

He danced a little jig.

"But why?"

She had come down step by step and unlocked her own door. "Who are you?"

"I'm my mother's child."

"What and why are you doing this? For fun?"

He pulled out a zip blade knife. "I'm a better actor than them.''

"How long have you known?"

"Know what? I have a message from my sister to kill you. To get it over with. You remember my sister?"

The words got stuck in her throat. "No, I never met your sister, Leroy. You know I didn't. Who was your sister?" Keep them talking. First rule of survival. "Leroy, what is this about? You live next door."

"But I have to kill you."

"Who?" She scrunched up her face. "Think who told you?"

He looked unsure of himself, lowering the knife, lifting the knife angrily. "My sister is a ghost."

"C'mon, Leroy give me the knife. C'mon."

"No, it's mine to kill with. I'm not Leroy. I'm Christopher S. Lane. Professor Lane to you."

"So it was you all along."

"No, it wasn't me." He did a little jig and stumbled.

"But who was it then?" She felt a twist of nausea.

"It was my sister. My brother-in-law killed them both with a gun. You are in cahoots with them. So you must be killed."

"But Leroy, they are dead. If you're Christopher Lane, you have to tell me why you are and what did he do?"

At the mention of Christopher Lane, she felt the knife nick her wrist and the pain and the bleeding that dripped like a faucet on the floor.

"Christopher Lane was a beloved drama professor who tried to get his doctorate three times and never got it, all three times, and was drunk early in the morning. Naughty boy."

B.J. wanted to stop the bleeding and be alone. He would go nick by nick until he carved her up and for what?

So it was him all along.

IT had started to rain now but only a warm drizzle. He reached the row of pink stucco houses and knocked at an open screen door. "Oh, excuse me, I'm looking for Number 2, Hall Street. Debbie Newsom Turk."

A woman stood with a frying pan, pregnant, and laughed.

"Don't pay it any mind, sir. She lives next door."

He also was dressed in the same clothes too long. His tie was open at the neck. His briefcase had collected some dust in this sleepy, dusty town. "Thanks," he said.

"Don't think you'll find her home."

The Breeding Years he thought. All the neighbors about the same age. The soggy grass was wet and his shoes were wet and muddy. He looked at his watch. She had to be home, otherwise he would lose the story line. Would he come back? Impossible.

He saw the house. All the lawns and backdoors were peppered with look-a-like toys. Bicycles, tricycles, baby dolls with chiseled China-doll looks, here and there a wagon. But they all looked alike. Joe saw this and then the flamingo on the screen door. It sure didn't look like they were home.

And then he saw it—a white nylon curtain open and

then close. Then a boy's voice. "Maaaa-me. We got ourselves some company."

Then the wait and the timing when he pulled out his Press Card. She felt trapped and then opened the door for the handsome stranger. "Well, I'll never guess what this is about," the young pregnant woman said. "C'mon into the kitchen then, if you have to. Thought you gave up on stories about her."

They went into the kitchen and he saw a once-pretty now-attractive woman. She scooped up the baby who was running across the floor on his little tummy. And Joe felt his heart lurch. He was face-to-face with a little boy just a little younger than the picture on his desk.

"This here's Johnny. He's got one thing on his little mind. I have some candy and I didn't give him any. And he ain't getting any either. Isn't that right? I've got lunch ready, if you want somethin' good and speedy. Now what is it that you want?"

"Well, I'm calling today about B.J. Stronger, who calls herself Barbara Marshall."

"That's a nice name, but not the one she was born with. Why does she need a fake name?" Then she figured it out and nodded.

"Ward, boy, go downstairs and study for that math test." She put the baby on the floor and he was swishing back and forth, crawling toward the candy. She laughed. "Excuse me. Now damned if that ain't funny. I put the wrapped hard candies in the dish knowing the baby wouldn't want any. Not so much to go all the way into the closed parlor."

Joe smiled. Another boy came in through the door. "Etta Lee says that I'm a snot-nosed brat."

"Well, maybe you are."

"And she won't play with me anymore."

"Well, play with your sister then, maybe she'll stop jumping all over the house. And tell her me and her daddy got to figure out when she can take them ballet lessons.

"If you picked this house, stranger, to make it easy on yourself, forget it.

"I guess you want to know about B.J. I read this much of a column on her in the *Madison Free Press*. What did you say your name was?" He took out his card and gave it to her. "Is that where she finally settled? Well, Athens, Ohio. Is that a nice place to live?"

"Maaaa?"

"Yeah, Jeannie."

"Can I have a cookie?"

"No, darlin' it's right before lunch. Stay if you like."

"No, I have to get back to Athens, thanks. Catch a plane."

"Okay, I'll give it to you straight. None of the Townies were allowed to baby-sit for years afterward. We were blacklisted, you might say, while the Summers got the jobs or they brought out girls with them for the summer."

"So about the trial."

"What about the trial? Jeannie, you stop smacking your brother around or there'll be no cookie. Listen, mister, what are you after?"

"I'm writing a book called *Famous Trials in History*. I don't think she was guilty. And then, I'm not sure."

"Well, don't you journalism folks get all your facts and then let the reader figure it out?"

He studied the floor; the now docile baby who looked up at him grinned toothlessly.

"Maaa." Ward came running up from his downstairs study hall. "I'm stuck."

"Okay, go on to another problem. Wait until Daddy comes homes. And you, any questions?" Joe was thinking this might have been B.J.'s life. Maybe this was what she wanted. Something he wasn't ready for.

"Well, did Hughie go to the door that night in the

rain or didn't he? Why did he change his mind that fast? Or was he lying?''

"Whoooaaa, one question at a time."

"Well . . . ?"

She was jiggling the baby. "Face it. You love your baby, can you imagine what that was like? And then this gorgeous thing comes in, and in one night your baby isn't anymore. Your wife turns into a junkie for prescription pills. But the baby. Can you imagine feeling that? I don't know if you've been married or what, Mr. Peterson, but can you imagine what that must have felt like for poor Mrs. Jorrish? That was her name, wasn't it?"

Joe was beginning to feel uncomfortable.

"I mean how would you feel if your baby was murdered?" Joe swallowed hard, knowing his eyes were beginning to mist over.

"And the trial?" he said in a thin voice. "How come Hughie didn't answer about his whereabouts the night before?"

"There are people, Mr. Peterson, who don't answer. Nothin' to nobody. He didn't answer. They checked out his alibi with his parents. So he lied for a second, for a minute, forever. We never hear from Hughie, mister, or any of the Summers. Most of the Townies settled into life right here in Madison, which is nothing more, nothing less than you see. I married Frankie. Yes, I knew he was sweet on B.J., who was my best friend, so in a way I guess I hated her. Because I was stuck on Frankie, I both liked her and hated myself for hating her. Given her upbringing and all.

"Well, I wish you well. Sure you won't stay to lunch?" Joe shook his head. All the kids were around her, the little girl sucking her thumb. She was holding the blue-eyed blond baby.

"No. I have a plane to catch."

"And what if you never find out whether she was

178

innocent or she was guilty? I take it you're sweet on her. Listen here, she's lucky if she gets you, but that's what love is. It isn't some pleasant little fairy tale I do for the kids. Love is pain sometimes. Maybe you'll never know."

Joe skidded down the step and stumbled over some roller skates. He had come to take charge of the interview and get some real facts. Instead he came away with "Maybe you'll never know."

"WHAT are you waiting for?"

Leroy walked briskly around the room. "I was living next door at the time. I rigged the upstairs to sound like a ghost's haunt. And then they would stay downstairs, remember the story, and leave.

"But you stayed."

If only he would stop hopping around. B.J. figured she could take this tall string bean of a man in seconds. But she would be likely to kill him and they would come and blame her for another murder. Try to stay alive. Keep him talking, keep his deranged mind from spacing out. Now where did she know that from? From television. They all watched murder and cops and rolled on the floor laughing because of the unreality of it all. What would Bubbles do in this sitcom? Keep 'em talking until you own it.

"So Christopher Lang failed to get a doctorate in doctoring? I don't understand—oh no, a professor in mathematics."

"In dramatics, I was Mr. Lane then and everybody loved me but I loved the booze a little more."

"So you got fired?"

"Something like that. I came drunk to school and they asked for my resignation."

And why are you killing me?

Because I don't deserve to live?

She didn't ask him that.

179

"You look like someone," she said, edging up to the paper toweling, the knife held behind her back.

"Forget it, you're not going to live. You're taking up precious space, Barbara. Is that a made-up name, kiddo? Me thinks it has the ring of a lie. But afterwards you get used to it. And when you get used to it, you make the transition from someone who had everything to live for to someone who has to die. I decided to kill you instead of me."

"You'll never get away with it." Just keep talking and you won't be scared.

Another voice in the room. He dropped the knife. "Hi. Gourmet-to-Go! If that half-assed vulture doesn't leave in a minute I will kill the both of you. Come out and find a bottle of rum and there's always that chocolate stuff for your cereal. Liqueur. Listen, you alkie, get out. I'll kill you both, I don't care."

# Chapter Nineteen

LEROY, Christopher S. Lane, dropped his knife and ran out the door. How did he know about that. *How?* How did he know about his Fruit Loops and his chocolate joy juice?

He ran out and she ran to fix the door and then there was a scream outside. Or had she imagined it? She knew the one place to hide was in the bathroom sitting on the top of the toilet seat, her knife behind her back.

So there was another killer who wasn't responsible for that poor man next door. Where had he made that phone call from? Where? He must have gone next door. This person already knew the phone number.

This person was a killer. And Christopher. Only the town's most respected drunk. But now she was in a hell. Quickly she checked the bathroom window to see if she could crawl out.

She heard the door creep open and got up and stood on the toilet seat, starting to open the little window. There wasn't a sound in the house. Maybe it was a joke. Why was her house without a noise? Then it came, quietly, like a ghost: "Someone's hiding in the bathroom." And then a gunshot and then, unable to stand the terror, she came out into the apartment with a quick intake of breath.

All the lights were off. In the dim light she made out a black hood like an executioner's.

"Have you ever played Russian roulette?"

The voice.

Familiar.

She screamed.

The gun fired again.

There was no place to hide. Keep on talking. No one there but the killer, who lifted his hood.

Suddenly, her voice climbed higher and she was as she had been ten years ago. "Please Mr. Jorrish. I didn't kill your baby. I didn't."

No disguise of his voice. "A court of law found you guilty, so don't try one of your girlhood lies."

"Why? Mr. Jorrish? Why?"

She was crying now.

"Still beautiful, I see. Less beautiful with knife strokes tattooing your face. Do you want to know why? I'll tell you why, it's simple. 'An eye for an eye, an arm for an arm,' you see? And you defending and arguing for your life. There's a certain beauty to it, don't you see? I've been waiting for ten years to do this. Don't you see? Now I'll feel good about myself. I'll really be able to sleep. I will do the right thing."

"Yes, the right thing for you. But what about your family? Mr. Jorrish, do you know what it's like—prison. You'll be treated like an animal."

"I don't intend to get caught," he said and smiled.

HE stopped at the airport's phone and felt he should call her. He took out some change and waited for the rings. One-two-three-four. And the message, "Hi, this is Gourmet to Go." That's when he hung up.

All of a sudden he felt guilty. For opening old wounds. For spying on her behind her back. For what Debbie had said. For better or worse. That's what love was.

Joe bought a Snickers and browsed among the paperback titles with their raised gold and silver lettering. His book when he finished it would probably be hardcover. Almost literature. And then they would sell it to paperback. If he ever finished it.

THE shadows diminished to a twilight. He knew immediately someone mortal or human had been in his kitchenette. They had used the phone and left the receiver off the hook. That's why he lived alone and that meant it wasn't a spook.

Someone is killing her.

It should have been him. But it was someone else.

Someone should know. All that blood. He was about to reach for another drink but instead he went out to his car. Tell the police? Never. But that boyfriend of hers. Now, that wouldn't be yesterday's news. He turned the ignition in the car, thinking how it had become dark so early.

HE had picked up three or four detective paperback novels. He liked a fast-speed thriller and if he could get a cop as writer, all the better. Police procedurals. He would open them on the days he allowed himself a long lunch hour.

Today, he would fall way behind. Might as well splurge on some of them. He picked up a book called *The Babysitter.* With raised red lettering stretching to a drop of blood. Shock graphics. Mild title. Big book. Not right now. He stopped to have a drink at the bar and thought, "Nice try, Joe. Nice try."

He looked down at the four books and then went back to buy the fifth. *The Babysitter.*

# Chapter Twenty

SHE heard the voice but the room was quiet. He was dressed in black and except for the front door everything was locked. "How did you get in?"

"Back door just closed, not locked."

Leroy did that.

She felt her voice, the pleading, young voice, the seventeen-year-old. "Please, Mr. J. I want to live."

"Forget it. Though I'll give you a few choices. We can go out into that yummy blackberry bush and when your skin is all stained and scratched I'll just end your life with one gunshot to the forehead. Now, if you're lucky you'll die or if not you'll surely live like a vegetable. What about your lover boy then, how about that, Barbara Marshall?

"Or I could strangle you. That's my specialty.

"Or right in the old home by the range. Or here, murdered in cold blood. Maybe hot lips can find you here."

IT was after nine and Joe Peterson felt like he'd been to the dry cleaner's. How many more men would she fool? He fastened his seat buckle and *The Babysitter* fell across his lap.

Now what was he supposed to do?

He knew who she was. His old buddy had blown her cover. This wasn't the fresh little girl next door. Although she looked like it—that blond hair, blue eyes, and black sooty eyelashes. No makeup. She wore no makeup though he wished she'd use just a light lipstick and some blusher. That would do it. Then she would stop traffic.

He couldn't go home after this. Never when he was at the *Post* did he drink alone. He couldn't go home alone. Maybe he would break his rule and call her. Break his rule. He had already called her from the airport and she wasn't there. Out delivering an order for a party.

Nothing to worry about.

He could call her tomorrow and they would talk then.

About everything and nothing.

The plane landed; he stepped into his car, which he had left at the airport, and drove the long and twisty hills and roads to Athens.

Tomorrow he'd handle it. Tonight he would get pissy-eyed drunk.


HE had driven up and said to the secretary in the office, "I have a message for Joe Peterson." She turned toward the man who looked a little ragged.

"He's out of town."

She wanted to go home. It was a little blowy out.

"When did he say he'd come back?"

"Didn't," she said. And why don't you leave, he read in her eyes.

Turning, he headed toward the gin mill. Nice try.


"MR. Jorrish, you have no idea what you are doing to your family, really you don't. Please sit down and think this over. It's a selfish move. It won't bring back Joshua. Your wife will suffer and your little girl." PLEASE, MR. J., DON'T KILL ME.

185

He laughed and then twirled his gun playfully.

"And prison, Mr. Jorrish. Prison is like a half-life. I know, I did it for ten years. It seems like ten years of eternity."

"Don't talk, just appreciate the situation. You who spent ten years in jail for a crime you committed are trying to talk me out of a crime I want to commit. Because mainly this has haunted me, driven me to a locked-up space with my wife and lovely young daughter." He laughed a deep laugh.

"You did commit that murder?"

There was a hush.

Finally a whispered "I did not."

"Oh, really?" Again he twirled the gun like a Western movie on TV. "How can I be so sure? So it's you that has the last word on this?" He leaned closer and B.J. sucked her breath in so that she could hold perfectly still. Because any one thing would make her explode. Or one thing would make his finger press the trigger. "No, I asked a leading psychiatrist about this phantom killer versus the real one that was never seen, never witnessed, never caught. He said you brought in that fantasy killer."

For ten years he had wanted to tell that to her or had wanted it written up in the newspaper to heighten the scandal. Now he had told someone, namely her, and it wasn't enough. It was just not enough. Nothing was enough.

JOE Peterson drove right from the airport to his rock, his salvation, his office. He felt depressed, couldn't remember feeling as depressed except for after the shock had worn off of his wife and boy being dead because of somebody who didn't give a damn. He couldn't go back to his apartment. Not just yet could he face that lonely cage. He looked at his watch and then he checked under E in his files for Extra Scotch. Nothing. Might

186

as well go to the gin mill. They didn't fit in with him and he didn't exactly understand them, town workers most of them. There was a more suburban bar in Athens, Ohio. Made up of middle-class white-collar drinkers. He preferred the gin mill next to his office. He liked to drink with men who had dirty fingernails.

Using their language, he knew he would tell himself what he needed to hear tonight. Jail, prison, all total ten years. Whatever you say, the lady's an ex-con. And you know how ex-cons are, they end up back in the slammer.

That's what they would say if anyone knew his problem. Their problems were easy. "Wife's taken a fancy to the electric man. He read the meter and they've been seeing each other while the kids are watching. And my girl, shacked up instead of doing her homework, the kid's pregnant, not even seventeen yet, and I had to go blowing my mouth off about anti-abortion. Now I think she should have one and put this all past her. I mean I would pay for it but no one asks me. Because it's like I don't live there. You understand, don't you? Here, have a drink on me."

He sat on a stool and he watched Johnny Carson make a cutesy face. Suddenly he got the feeling that his right shoulder was being tapped. He turned. "Excuse me, are you Joe Peterson, the owner of the paper?"

THEY were out by the blackberry patch. He had the gun in her side; cool, still night almost liquid like icy water, black-midnight water.

She thought of terrorists and their hostages. They didn't have to kill. They were ordered to do it. Just as Mr. Jorrish's voice was telling him what to do, what to say. It must be nice to have a voice.

"On second thought," he said, and B.J. shrank from

187

the noise, the intrusion on her private thoughts, the rain beating on her eyelashes.

"Yes?" she said hopefully. She had to go to the bathroom but it was silly to ask now. After she was dead she wouldn't have that feeling.

"Some blackberries?" he asked. Not unless she could crumble them in her hands and decorate his face with war paint. Just squish it on like feces.

"After you, my dear. Did you rehearse this with anyone before I showed up?" If only she could make herself as crazy as he was. It was eleven-thirty. Would she be dead before midnight? She closed her eyes and prayed for just another day. Just a few more hours.

"THE answer is if you want a special story or need me for a favor, then I'm not home, understand? But if you're giving me something, like a scoop, or a whatchamecallit, then I'll take it. Free."

"I think your girlfriend is in trouble."

Joe spun around. "Who's my girlfriend?"

"Barbara Marshall. Lives right next door to me. I would run to help her if I were you. I really would."

"What kind of trouble?"

"I'll tell you later. Just pay the man, can you walk?"

"God, I got drunk. Too many beers and whiskies."

"C'mon, man, you're okay, pay the man, leave a tip. Now, where's your car?"

"It's at the paper."

"Never mind, we'll take mine. On second thought, you're not fit to drive tonight. And believe me, I know. Oh yes, I know those empty nights when booze fills it. That's why you should carry . . . where's the car . . . okay carry on and I'll drive you there."

"Shouldn't we call the police?"

"We may have to do that, but I would say there's a girl in a very bad spot. Life or death."

They got into his car, which rattled and chugged along as if it had pneumonia.

Mile by mile, Joe could feel himself sober up. He didn't know that much about the man. In New York, this would be a hit but now he was wondering if there was something wrong with the man. He wasn't drunk but he had bats in his belfry somehow.

"Oh, damn, damn, I went down the wrong road. I seem to be doing worse without the booze. Ever have fruit loops and red wine for breakfast. That's the pits, man, really low down."

THEY were back in the apartment now. With B.J. still pleading and Joshua Jorrish's father happier than he'd been in a long time. All of a sudden, something happened so fast that she ducked and Mr. Jorrish was tackled down. He put his head down and fired toward the ceiling and then fired again and dropped it.

"Oh my God, I almost killed you, Rachael."

It was dark in the room. B.J. sat on the floor trying hard not to pee in her pants.

B.J. watched them in the dark. Who had put this pain in all their lives? It was unbearable. Maybe Rachael would shoot her.

"Come back home, Tom. Tommy. We'll call Dr. T. and he'll make everything all right for you again. Let it go, dear, let it go. She hurts us at every turn but let it go. Look, it's made you sick again."

Tom Jorrish was still sobbing. "I could have killed you, Rachael. Then there would be no one to share what the good times were."

"We'll make more good times. Who knows? Maybe we could adopt another child? Wouldn't that be a good time? Maybe that would help Jessica. Her therapist said that to me: 'Have you ever considered?' We'll make a list and entitle it, Have You Ever Considered."

"Oh, Rachael, I almost lost you, me with my lousy temper."

Rachael turned around and found B.J., who had put her skirt over her head and was sitting like an upside-down flower.

"I don't want you to think we don't blame you for everything that's wrong in our lives, because we do blame you, but it's that . . . well, I—" Rachael's voice broke. "Don't you think I don't wish we could do it. That we don't think your getting out in ten years was slightly to the left of liberal. I wish he had been able to pull something off. But the fact is, I don't want you ruining my life any more than you already have. First our baby, and now my husband. Prison would kill him, did you ever think of that?"

Then as the folds of her skirt fell back again, B.J. sat back. It was over. The man and the woman were leaving. She folded her head and made a pillow of her elbows and fell asleep on the floor, knowing she was safe, had gotten a second chance at life.

WHEN the car pulled up B.J. was sound asleep on the floor and Joe and Leroy could see the wreck of the living room.

"Whatever happened, I don't think we'll know yet the full account. God, is she out cold?"

He picked up her head and stooped down so she was curled into his lap.

"B—Barbara? Are you okay? Maybe we should call a doctor?"

"No, she's okay, in shock though."

"Should we leave her here?" Joe asked Leroy. Then he answered his own question. "No, I know what she needs. She needs not to witness other people's horrors, you know what I mean?"

"Not exactly, but maybe she needs to sleep in her own bed. C'mon, let's lead her."

190

They each held her, an arm under an armpit as B.J. resisted them, crying softly. "No more."

"Okay, Barbara, this is your bedroom."

She became alarmed. Who was Barbara? Not her name.

"No one's going to hurt you. Take off all your clothes and leave them in a pile."

She looked past him and burst into tears.

"Barbara," Joe said, "can you hear me?"

She shook her head no.

Joe laughed. "Oh, you goofball, you'll be fine. Nobody's going to hurt you, you'll be okay. B—Barbara? Yo, Leroy?"

"Yes." He stood in the shadows.

"Can you stay?"

"Yes. I was thinking I could put cardboard in this window that's been broken." Knowing a little bit of her history, Joe said, "I don't think we should bring this to the attention of the police."

At the word *police*, B.J. started to cry and pound the bed.

"No police. Do what you think, Leroy. You're a good man. Too good for fruit loops and wine. Of course, maybe shredded wheat and gin might be better.

"Did you do what I told you to do?"

As she carefully bundled up her clothes and held them in front of her he could see how scared she was and how used to taking orders. His heart broke in two.

"Here. Put your hair up." He handed her a barrette. For a while she deliberated whether to drop her clothes and put her hair up or put the barrette in her mouth for later.

"Come, come, I'm falling asleep looking at you. Let's have yourself a nice bath. Do you have any bubble bath?"

The barrette clamped in her mouth made her answer unintelligible. "Mfdfgit Sayth?"

191

"Right. Do you have anything feminine, frothy, relaxing, something with perfume?"

She stared at him.

"Oh, I know just what this needs." He ran into the kitchen, then ran back and started the bathwater running. She was falling asleep against the door, half watching him.

He put something in the bathwater and watched it bubble. "Okay, step in. I'll look the other way. Okay, because we're not going to be spending the whole night in the bath. I want you to eat a little, not a lot. God, I would kill for a cigarette."

At the word *kill*, B.J. backed up and whimpered, "I didn't do it, Mr. Jorrish, really I didn't. Please don't kill me, please. I want to live."

"Oh, you're a heartbreaker, aren't you?" he said but he was afraid he would start crying himself.

She eased into the bath and then let herself enjoy it. She picked the bubbles out from in between her feet. It was as if she had never taken a bath before.

"Scrub the dirt, Sleeping Beauty. Under the nails, under the toe nails, between the toes. And you know where and you know how."

He disappeared for a minute and went out quickly to see how Leroy was doing. He had sealed in some cardboard and pasted it up. Then he ran back into the bathroom and found B.J. nodding off, almost ready to slip under.

He laughed and pulled her out. "Don't drown, not after all we've done here.

"But it's nice, huh? Okay, next question. Do you possibly have a nightgown, dress, something that makes you feel cozy and feminine? Barbara, you can get out of the tub."

She got out, hugged him fiercely, leaving an outline of her body on his suit and shirt. He swatted her on her behind and quickly handed her a towel.

"Anything to eat in that fancy refrigerator? Anything edible?"

Leroy opened the door. "Naw, cake batter, no eggs, green icing, gum drops."

"Nothing edible."

"Listen, sport, wait a minute." He stopped and began to wipe B.J.'s back with her towel. "Now go get your jammies or whatever you wear."

"Do you have a beer in your house?" he asked Leroy.

"Is the Pope a Catholic?"

"Just one beer, we don't need any more than one. That will let her relax. Not that she's not doing a good job of it herself."

He found her lying over the covers, a flannel nightgown on her smelling like Joy detergent. He smiled and let her lie there for a while. Then he found a brush and, taking out the clip, he began to brush her hair.

Leroy was back in a minute with the beer.

"Big beer drinker, aren't you, Barbara?"

She nodded peacefully, smiling, although she didn't lift her head off the pillow.

"We need food. And someone should stay inside with this one. She looks like a sleepwalker. You know what I'm thinking? Some burgers, some french fries, some cokes and some shakes, chocolate and just pig out on that. Here's a twenty, go for broke."

Leroy saluted and let a little moonlight into the kitchen. "Good man, you are," said Joe. "How about reviewing the little theater in the area and also movies? If you'd like the job, you've got it."

Joe looked down. She was so gorgeous, it was enough to make your head spin.

He let her doze for a while and then walked around the living room. Two couches facing each other, a coffee table in between, a step up and then the practically full kitchen on the top from side to side and a small bathroom with a sink on the left side and to the right a full bathroom with shower and tub. He could tell she didn't spend much time in the living room. No, it was the kitchen that got all the action.

The couches were nice. Kind of a light pearlized blue or blue grey with big soft pillows. One would need to memorize the whole room, layout of the apartment to be really effective if the time ever came.

When Leroy got back, they watched her snarf down the cheeseburger, the fries, and the chocolate milk shake. She burped and he handed her the beer. "Drink this, B—Barbara." Damn, it was getting harder and harder to carry on the charade, but if he slipped once with her, she wouldn't trust him anymore.

"I have her keys, a full set," Leroy said.

"How cozy."

"Best to leave them somewhere and she'll find them. Nah, on second thought I should hold her keys. In case of emergency."

"Here, Barbara, now you should go to bed. We're going to lock you in here, will you be okay?"

She smiled at him and reached to kiss him on the cheek. He wanted with all his heart to sleep on one of the cushions on top of the twin couches. Instead, he helped her into the little bedroom with the twin bed, dresser, and closet. A small room, almost an afterthought, but perfect for the single girl.

"Unplug the machine. They can save it for three days."

Then Joe looked at her. How many times had she pulled the plug? How many people were after her with grudges? Silently he recalled the people he talked to.

No one was openly hostile.

But they hated her anyway. Each one was hostile to her. Who would try to kill her? It would come to him. Right now they needed to get out and let her sleep.

B.J. fell on top of the bed, face away from the wall.

194

And he could see by the look on her worried face that she was reliving every nightmare she'd had from the age of three.

"Aw, I can't leave you like this."

He spotted a spare pillow. "Okay, here's your extra pillow. Sleep on one and hold the other, cuddle it."

As if by an artist, the frown was erased, a single stroke turning it into a smile. "Okay, think it's safe to leave her?"

Leroy smiled. "I still live across the yard in an almost identical duplex house. No one will come anymore. I think her nightmare is finished. Tonight I'm pouring all my stuff down the drain, you can count on me."

"And your articles. What will you call yourself?"

"Christopher S. Lane."

"Good man, Chris. I'm going home to catch forty winks. Or it looks like four winks, I don't know. Where'd they get such a stupid expression?"

"Or in the Land of Nod."

"Yeah, I used to be this sophisticated New Yorker. Another one I particularly hate is 'Beautiful Baby-sitter.'"

"I know what you mean," Leroy said and the full moon hung in the sky, lighting up the driveway between the two almost identical houses.

Leroy took him home. Sometime when he got home, the moon lifted and everything looked like this shiny pink sheen. When he let himself in, he looked at his empty half-made bed, and, taking his suit jacket and pants off, just fell on the bed. He thought of her for a second. Orphaned, raised by grandparents, jailed before she became a woman. The Beautiful Baby-sitter. He was surprised she hadn't got book offers before she got out. But, oh yes, she would plead her story of innocence. Look at Jean Harris, both with their dishy looks.

He willed himself to sleep even if he had a hard time trying to figure out which one of the cast members in the play had made her life a misery. That wasn't hard. There were Ohio license plates in the driveway. The Jorrishes had left a car. No, that wasn't hard. She was safe now, her would-be killers tucked in somewhere else.

IN Athens, B.J. got up, put on her bathrobe and walked through her house. She was free. It was all a little hazy and hard to remember but she was free. She could take up her catering business now. And Joe, she would never forget how he took care of her. She came out and sat down and finished a container of french fries.

ACROSS the driveway, Leroy poked around for a snack before he went to bed. There were the Fruit Loops. He looked wistfully at the stash he had picked up. Now, how would he eat his Fruit Loops? He looked longingly at the red wine. And then he found something tucked inside. A bottle of milk. He poured himself a toast. But then he caught himself. He had almost killed her. And for what? Because he was crazy after all these years, God help him.

# Chapter Twenty-One

Two days later, with Leroy and Joe still secretly acting as bodyguards, the phone rang in B.J.'s machine. She had learned to screen her phone calls by picking up after the person announced who it was.

It was another order. A birthday party, a sweet-sixteen party for one of the professors' children, the oldest girl.

B.J. had learned to quiz the anxious mother for the child's hobbies or special interests. This little girl liked to jog. The birthday party in three days. No problem. She had her life back again. "He" hadn't called but he must be very busy after she kept them both up that night. She wouldn't talk about it or mention it. Tom and Rachael, they had done it. Their car was gone. They were gone. It was over.

Leroy tapped at her screen door and she opened it. "Listen," he said, "Mrs. Panny isn't going to fix that screen door. Let me fix that for you."

"Oh, that would be great," she said in her breathy little-girl voice that reminded him of Marilyn Monroe or Jacqueline Onassis.

He fixed the broken screen door and then pointed to the window. "Have that fixed before it gets cold, I promise. Have to measure your window."

"Let me get you some money."

"This is a treat. It's on Mr. Peterson of the *Voice*. He said make sure you use it. There are some crazy loons around this part of the country." His face blushed a deep red and he vanished.

In his circa 1949 manual typewriter was a review he was writing of a movie he had seen. Hell, he would pan it, that would make more people want to see it anyway. He had said the sex was in poor taste and the theater owner would applaud it.

"SONUVABITCH!" Joe screamed as he picked up the phone in his office. "How the hell are you? Yeah, I got those clippings."

"So did it do anything for you, to you, give you a hard-on? Did you rip them up and you hate my guts? Don't you think I called you to ask how fast you can pick up your things and get on a plane and come home?"

"The thing of it buddy is we don't want you throwing away your life like that—a little too harsh."

"Nasty, Irv, but caring. Well, I can't say much, except life goes on. Hired a movie and theater reviewer."

"Wait a second, do they have movies in a town that size?"

"Gimme a break, pal. Just gimme a break. When are you coming down for another day of fishing, canoeing, what else?"

They kept the bantering up until his secretary buzzed him. Without a break, leaving his old buddy talking, he answered her.

"How are you doing? Listen I'm on a phone call. Can you hold for a minute?" Suddenly the sunshine over the garden out back was a little more sparkling and the birds in the trees a little sweeter sounding.

He came back on the line with his old buddy, who hadn't even noticed he was missing.

"Listen, old buddy, can I call you back real soon? She's on another line."

"*She*'s on the other line? You don't quit. Sonuva-bitch. Okay, buddy, I won't hold you not if it's *she*. Stay in touch, Joe."

"Well, well, how's Sleeping Beauty?" he said. He didn't really know what to say now. Maybe she never wanted to see him again because he had to be so bossy.

"I just wanted to thank you for all you've done."

I *just* wanted to thank you?

"Well, why don't you do a little more?"

So they would mention nothing of the incident. Or the key players. And then he had to remind himself it was none of his business. It was over. Someone had done something terrible to her and scared now-reformed Leroy Phillips back to Christopher S. Lane, III, or was it II? Anyway he was on the wagon and not off the wall. The two of them and the secretary were the only paid employees. He had organized a carload of little boys to sell it but they came and went. Sometimes he drove the van himself and tossed the paper.

"Listen, I have an idea. Since we're both pressed for time, let's take an hour break and have a picnic."

"A picnic!" She couldn't help laughing. "You want a picnic?" He could tell she was laughing so hard the tears were rolling down her eyes.

"Yes, you'll pack a basket and we'll go to this grassy knoll I have in mind and throw all the food away and just neck."

"What kind of food on this catered lunch?" she asked.

"Oh, you know—just scavange, take a little from this one and take a little from this one. Don't put yourself out."

She giggled. "Sounds great. As long as we're both busy."

199

"And I'll bring the wine. I have a nice Chablis."
He reached over to his file drawer and looked under
Wine. "Yep, a nice white wine. You bring the rest and
I'll pay you for it."

"You don't have to do that."

"No, no, my treat. And I'm going to ask you to pick
me up at the paper. Okay?"

"Sounds great!"

# Chapter Twenty-Two

THE day was beautiful. Even the tar on the dirt road in front of her house smelled pungent. Early fall, late summer, almost like spring. B.J. giggled as she got into the van and drove over to the highway to get some junk food. Hamburgers, cheeseburgers, french fries, and nothing but white wine. She had never had white wine.

The rain had stopped. There was a whitish aura in the countryside and the ground was hard and springy again. The rain had stopped, finally.

But the weather forecaster was predicting rain on the little radio she kept going in the kitchen. One day she would buy her own TV set, color. Leroy had fixed the screen door. She could relax. Or she *would* feel relaxed except for the fact that she was having lunch with him. But only lunch. Somehow that made it better.

He had only two ads to write before she picked him up. He was the chief copywriter for his clients. For a hardware store and a lumber company. He chewed on his pencil and came up with "We sell hardware like you buy software." And for the lumber company "Whatever you're building, start it with Laneway." Start it with Laneway. Start it with Laneway. Get a good foundation with Laneway?

She decided she wanted something gourmet. She stopped at a farmer's market and bought some brie and swiss. And some fruit—black grapes, soft pears. She grabbed a carrot cake from the backseat.

She drove through town and marveled at how much it could sub for being a small Western town like the ones on television. Horses in front of a hitching post, and the women in long cornflower-blue dresses stopping in to shop for a bit of ribbon.

She wondered about the Jorrishes. She remembered only slightly what happened except Joe had been there and she felt like a little girl. And it was good. Because no one had treated her like that when she was little.

She couldn't say she was falling in love with him. Love, Bubbles told her, is when you care and share it. She didn't know how to care and how could she share her past with him? Never, so it would be lunches and movies and she would keep to herself. But now she had nothing to worry about. The Jorrishes were gone and he would get some help.

Here it was. The *Voice*. The *Salem Voice*.

He was waiting for her and she couldn't help but notice the baseball hat turned sideways and his suit-jacket in a little ball.

"Get in. I feel like I'm kidnapping you from the paper," she said and laughed.

He took her good looks in and noticed right away she was relaxed. She'd probably slept well for the first time since she moved into that booby trap. Haunted House, well he didn't know.

"How come the hat?"

He touched his Mets baseball cap he wore sideways. "Oh, only when I write copy for a client."

"What's 'copy'?"

"Oh, you know. The words that go with the pictures in an ad. Let's forget about business and have a good time. Okay?"

"Sure, lunch will be ready in two seconds."

They parked in a patch of green shielded by three weeping willows and off in the distance they heard the screams and cries of early football practice at Athens High.

She put the cheese and fruit on a small silver tray she had in the back of the van. She was wearing a white shirt and red pants and sneakers. He was wearing suspenders and his baseball cap. He had already started laughing when she took out a tray of Burger King bags.

"I thought you were going to do that."

They both started to laugh.

Then for a long while they both had the munchies.

"Busy at the paper?" she finally asked.

"Always busy at the paper. It's uncanny the way the light is tinting your hair. I mean, I already know you color your hair but why? It would look really good the natural color. Kind of tawny-colored, isn't it?"

B.J. began to blush and she stiffened perceptibly.

Cleaning off another cheeseburger, Joe made a little corner near a tree and propped up on that.

It was quiet. She said, "Blonds have more fun."

"Not always."

"I did bring deviled eggs."

"You little devil," he said, feeling himself succumb to the romance of the setting.

"Where did you find this spot?"

"Oh, it's an extension of Lover's Lane. I found it. The kids haven't caught on yet. Did you have a Lover's Lane in that place you're from? Where is it, Madison?" She felt a little more edgy. She hadn't talked to him about Madison. But he had got it somewhere. She must have mentioned it once or twice.

"Oh, I have done my share. There was no Lover's Lane. On the beach."

She stiffened again, sitting ramrod straight with her legs crossed. She dropped a french fry.

203

A buzzer went off in Joe's mind. Mistake. Error. Recompute. He wasn't supposed to know about Madison or Madison-on-the-Lake. But he did and he would slip more, he was sure. He wouldn't even attempt to call her "Barbara" because he would want to say "B.J." He liked that name more. She had never looked like a Barbara. And now he was messing up and she was upset. That look on her face, that haunted, hunted look.

"Sorry I didn't have time to bake a cake, I just grabbed a carrot cake."

"Oh, you shouldn't have bothered. But I'm glad you did." He grabbed her ankle and tickled her. "Say, are you having fun?"

"Nice break," she said, and Joe noticed that she now would get uptight. It was better when he didn't know. What good was useless information? She leaned back on the grass, pulled a long weed and used it like a toothpick. Who did that? Oh yes, how could he forget so quickly?

The brother.

But that was in Madison. Then it hit him. There were many ways that the two towns were similar. Midwestern. Small. Summer and college students versus Townies. Good touch.

"You're going to get grass stains all over that lovely shirt," he said to her.

"I'll wash it out," she said.

What was wrong with his tongue? He better just keep his mouth closed. There was nothing he said that was right.

She was thinking, He's under a lot of pressure, that's all. But her throat felt tight and she suddenly felt like crying. They didn't talk for a while and then when she closed her eyes and opened them she was looking up into his brown, velvety eyes as he kissed her.

She sat up as she said, "I better be going back to

work, don't you think?'' Uptight gave way to prissy and uptight. No wonder she didn't want to use Lover's Lane like it was meant to be, he had done nothing but insult her. His way of punishing her, he guessed, and again heard the voice of Debbie: *You may never know.* And he had fished for clues.

"Yeah, let's clean it up. Looks like there's an ugly storm coming our way.''

B.J. tightened up. "Too much rain,'' she said.

"No, actually, it's welcome. We're in a drought, don't you have a radio?''

"Oh,'' she said.

Lover's Lane, he thought, but she was younger than her years. Yes, he figured. In some ways. And in other ways she was older and wiser. Some friendship for her. He wished he could rewind the clock and leave out some of his questions. He plopped his cap back on, threw his jacket over his shoulder.

"Looks like we'd better go home and batten down the hatches,'' he said. Finally a topic. "You know Leroy is working for me on a free-lance scale. He writes the reviews for little theaters and movies. I think he'll do all right by us. Later I can train him to be a reporter.

She said nothing but smiled at him. "That's nice.'' Privately she thought, *If you can keep him sober.*

They got into the van and drove back into town. He looked out his window and she looked straight ahead. "Got a lot of work,'' he said, not taking his eyes off the scenery, which was Athens Main Street. Suddenly he showed some interest. "Okay, kid, let me out here.'' He kissed her hurriedly, took off his cap, and put his jacket on. He was gone and she was still driving through the town, feeling like she needed a dessert and remembering that she baked them.

It was a nice lunch but something was wrong. Someday she'd figure it out but tonight she could get back to what she had to do. There was something she liked

205

about Joe. He respected her business. He always knew she had to work. Suddenly she found herself crying and she didn't know why. She fished with one hand for a kleenex in her bag and blew. Then she had this euphoria that she always had, knowing she was going to fill a whole order for a paying client and that she had this business she loved.

Everything would be all right. He didn't kiss her the first time. Again, she had this business. It was asking for too much. Yes, he had taken care of her without asking any questions and then he had been preoccupied. He was running a whole newspaper. And now Leroy Phillips, the new Leroy, was next door and she didn't have to be afraid of him anymore.

Just her business. That's all that mattered. She drove the rest of the way home, humming a tune. She liked that man and he was doing nothing to take her time. She was free and having fun.

As she got to the door she noticed the thing had been fixed on the screen door. She could tell that another storm was going to wash over them. As she went in, she realized she was already staggering under the load she had. Soon she'd be running an ad in the paper for a helper or a driver or whatever she needed. So it would be good to be snuggly and alone and working while the damn rain passed by.

More red blinking. More orders. She picked up her pencil. "B.J. Stronger. Thank you for having an answering machine. I'm the real killer but no one knows it. This is not a joke. It's the baby-killer. I'm not going to give you a chance to live."

# Chapter Twenty-Three

SHE probably would never want to see him again after that. Joe stood outside the offices of the *Salem Voice*. It had been the *Athens Chariot* when he bought it. Some of the townspeople who had lived there a zillion years couldn't get used to the new name or the new paper.

He squinted at his newspaper building in the sunshine that was left. It was another stormy night, maybe he should call and talk to her. He sure botched up lunch. She probably wouldn't want to go out with him again.

And besides there was THAT. Oh yes, there was that. And you didn't fool around where there was that obstacle. But he could call and apologize. He located a pay phone and tried to call. But the line was busy.

B.J. took the phone off the hook.

Then she staggered backward and shut the door. She ran to the windows and the front door.

Maybe it was a joke?

She trembled and sighed. The voice so disguised, so familiar.

Was the whole world waiting to kill her? Because she didn't know how many times she could defend herself before she just didn't care anymore.

It could be Joe. Second thoughts on the lunch was

that it wasn't fun. He had been testing her. Testing her for what?

She rewound it and played it again and knew she had never heard that voice in her life. It was muffled and greedy and sent her into her bedroom. Then she remembered something that she had forgot. The broken lock. Leroy had fixed it so she could lock or unlock it. She had forgotten it was not locked. Quickly she rushed there but it was too late.

# Chapter Twenty-Four

THE sound of the screaming frightened her. It was coming from her and from the person in the room, though he didn't move his lips. She had thought it was Joe. She leaned over, saw the black hair, and recognized it. She had looked up and saw the rubbery features and the hideous smile and saw the killer. After ten years she saw the killer and saw it was a mask.

"So we meet again," he said in a voice that started deep basso and ended in a high, birdlike voice. "Take your pick of my voices. I believe we can abstain from discussing your illustrious past."

He took off the stifling mask and threw it on the floor.

"Oh, God," she whispered, crying, taking small backward steps, inviting him in when he already was.

"It was you. I never thought it. But why, Willie, why go to this kind of trouble? You could have just killed me."

They both stared at the puddle, the face that looked like an organ grinder. It was on the floor. She looked at Willie and tried to find the boy when all she saw was the man. The killer.

She whispered to him, "Don't kill me, Willie. I'm so

tired. Everybody wants to kill me. No more, Willie. Don't kill me.''

"Don't call me 'Willie.' " His booming voice filled the space that had been quiet. That had been hers.

"Did you kill that baby, Wilton Stronger? Did you? Yes, I guess you did.''

"Listen, Betty Jo. Our grandparents are long gone. You can't kill kin, they would say. I hear their voices telling me what to do. And now they say, Find B.J. Wilton and do away with her.

"Now I can kill you because we have no kin. They say, Now, strike while the iron's hot. Grandmother told me that just lately.''

"Yes, I can just hear her say that. But, Willie, you don't take that literally. Please, Willie, don't kill me.'' She went back through the years. "Please, Willie, don't hit me anymore.''

"Don't call me 'Willie.' No one calls me that to my face anymore. I'm Wilton Stronger and I own half of Madison, Beej, that I do. No one would lock me up like we did to you. And all the time you were innocent. That's a laugh.''

He socked B.J. on the shoulder, almost dropping his gun.

She wondered then, as she had often thought, if he wasn't quite sane. Where was the sanity?

But Willie kept going. "The grandparents are long gone. The television set is off forever. In fact, I sold the house. They're tearing down the house and building a new one.''

She wanted to sit down but she was too mesmerized by her brother. And what was coming out of his mouth and the spell-binding realization that he was the murderer. That he had done it ten years ago. Snuffed out the baby's life and hers too.

"You can't kill kin," Wilton said. "Over and over they would say, 'Don't kill her, just get rid of her, she's standing in our way.' So I searched for a way." Then he jumped to the present. "That reporter guy worries me. Think B.J. Who's the reporter? Why is he so interested in your case?"

B.J. shivered. "What reporter guy?" He must mean Joe. He hadn't been interested. He just wanted a scoop, a story.

"Ever since your boyfriend interviewed me, Beej, I knew I had to hear it from you. And he told me where you were."

B.J. felt she would vomit. "Boyfriend? What boyfriend? I don't have any boyfriend." She knew those steely eyes, that tousled hair. He was ready for a fight. Had to have one and she knew it would be with Joe. But Joe had lied to her. She had thought so . . . much of him.

So she couldn't trust him. That's why the lunch had gone bad this afternoon.

"Turn on the light, B.J. You'll see me one more time." With the light on, she turned away; it was the same Willie, the same haircut combed a different way.

So Joe was never really interested in her. God, that hurt, he didn't care at all. Just research for a book or some articles. That's what writers were like. She was stupid to think otherwise. But she still did.

Then he shut off the lights. The rain started then, a torrent that splashed down, welcome rain, soothing rain.

"You don't like storms much, do you, B.J.?"

"I hate you."

"Now, don't get emotional. Who knows what might have happened with or without the storms? Careful, B.J., don't slip on the floor. Gourmet-to-Go. Gimme a break!"

"No, I was doing great before—before you came by."

"Gone-with-Gourmet, they'll call it. Careful, B.J.,

211

don't slip on the floor. It's going to be slippery with blood before we're finished tonight."

He turned the lights on and went to her kitchen. He took a knife out and he threw it on the floor. "Can you work that knife? Here, I'll give you a fighting chance."

The lights went out and they scrambled for the knife. Then Wilton had both a gun and the knife. The lightning and thunder frightened B.J. When the world turned upside down.

She heard a door open and flap shut and then flap open and shut for a little while. Something else the landlady should have fixed. Wilton took his gun and fired one shot in the air. He was breathing hard like a horse at the gate.

"Willie, I can't see you. Willie, please don't kill me, please. Our grandparents can see you from the grave. And so can our parents. Willie, are you listening?"

"Shut up, I hear you. But there's something wrong with this room. Let me think on it awhile."

"Oh, please, Willie, turn on the light. Go home, back to your family. Do you have a family?"

"Now, listen up, baby sister." She thought how often he had called her that. It had rhymed with baby-sitter, baby sister, baby-sitter, baby sister, baby . . .

"You ain't my baby sister anymore. You never were. The joke was on us. Our 'grandparents' had a child, a child that was theirs but they couldn't raise it without shame. They were past fifty. So I went to live with our parents. But they weren't my parents. Jesus, B.J., don't act so dumb. You're living in our world. I'm not your brother. And it was their idea to get rid of you."

"No, I don't believe it."

"You were always stupid and dense." Where was his voice? Follow the voice. The voice was slipping away.

"Skip to the part about the reporter. What does he know about us?"

"A lot. Forget him. I doubt if he's thinking of you now."

"What's the rest of the story, Wilton?" Just keep him talking, keep him talking, but this time she thought she had met her match. And she wouldn't put anything past him. Nothing.

"You had a fantastic, fabulouso Trust Fund."

She heard the sound of air being sliced with a knife.

"Got it, baby sister." Again she heard "baby-sitter."

"And there was about—oh, over, let's say of one-hundred and fifty thousand dollars. And we wanted you to give it over to us. And so I looked at the small print and found that it was given over to the next of kin if you were dead. If you were in a coma, or if you were incarcerated. Now the grandparents weren't going to allow me to kill you, so I devised this foolproof answer. I was going to kill the baby and end your life. Went without a hitch. One thing we didn't expect was your parole. New plan. Beautiful Baby-sitter Paroled—Killed by Boyfriend."

"Nobody will believe that," B.J. said, her voice cracked, tears rolling down her eyes.

"Oh, yeah, when we get through with you, B.J., we'll all but have him dead and buried. Smart fella. Knows too much. I'm running for office. State senate for a first. I don't need hangers-on like you or your dumb boyfriend."

She heard a couch tumble over and then two gun-shots.

"Duck!" someone whispered.

She went behind the nearest wall and stood up, holding on to it.

"C'mon, boy. Let's see your stuff," Willie hissed.

Another gunshot. Silence. One person breathing. Two people breathing.

She slinked into the kitchen and found a knife by the light of the lightning. Then she remembered how a storm could hide the noises. She could scream and no one would hear her, not even Leroy next door. There was another gunshot. B.J. was aware that her face was awash with tears.

She skidded, sliding on the wave of blood that washed her away and fell back. It was sticky and she thought she would be sick to her stomach.

It was black when one gun went off. There was a break and then she turned on the lights and screamed. Two bodies on the floor. One of them breathing heavily.

She turned off the light.

One of them was dead.

But somehow she had lived.

She was alive.

And then she admitted: what was the difference?

# Chapter Twenty-Five

"SAY, don't I know you from—"

The black woman gorgeously dressed said, "Don't give me that shit, baby, I'll cut your throat."

"Bubbles? Bubbles!" She heard her before she saw her. She was wearing a wig and high, high heels.

"Bubbles, don't you look fine."

"My man paid for all this. Listen, baby, sweetheart, listen to Bubbles, stand by your man and you'll live. Bubbles likes this man for you. Now how's he doing, sweetie? Look at this page.

"REPORTER FIGHTS FOR HIS LIFE AS HE SAVES SWEETHEART.

"And this one?

"CONVICTED KILLER FOUND INNOCENT.

"And this one I like the best.

"CONVICTED KILLER PROVED INNOCENT BY PRINCE CHARMING."

"He's okay, Bubbles, he calls me B.J. now."

"Oh, sure everything's going to be okay. You'll be fine. You might have children, did you ever think of that? I caught a look at him. He's a looker and he loves you, B.J. Now think on it, isn't this more than you thought you would ever be deserving of?"

"Oh, Bubbles." It was then she heard the gum. She

blew one purple bubble and then cracked it. They kissed and Bubbles left with her high-heel shoes clicking on the floor.

TOMORROW they would bury Wilton.

She stole a look at Joe, who was smiling at her. Soon, they would have the I.V. removed. He winked at her and she smiled at him.

"Who's Irwin Norris? He keeps calling."

"Oh, he keeps calling?"

"He says he wants to buy a carrot cake."

"And he probably does."

"Oh, Joe."

"Yes, B.J.?"

"Why didn't you say something? I don't know how you did this."

"Easy. I always follow a lead. Your brother, or whatever we're calling him, was living too high on the hog for where he had come from. So he had bought that used car lot from whom and with what? Then I talked to Debbie Newsom Turk."

"She married Frankie. Isn't that nice?"

"Yes, isn't that nice. She told me, B.J., that if I really loved you it wouldn't matter if you were innocent or not."

"My God, I spent ten years in jail for nothing."

He grabbed her arm, almost pinching it. "Listen, you grew up, you survived. Where would you be now?"

"I would be an actress and maybe a movie star."

"Is that what you want to do? I have some contacts that would help you along."

"No, that's not what I want to do." She kissed him on the forehead. "I want to be with you and help you with your paper and bake my carrot cakes. And I'm sure if you had a slice you'd feel much better. I should have had one for Bubbles. She always listened to my recipes in . . . in . . ."

"Prison," he said very softly. "That night in Madison I figured something out. Your brother had to have gotten a lot of money to have bought that used car lot. He had married a Madison girl but she was not rich at all, slightly poorer than Wilton. They had no children. So it didn't figure. But the night we were in your house, it figured. All of it figured. And I even had a witness in that room."

"Who was it?"

"Old Leroy. He slipped out the front door and called the police."

Just then a man in a corduroy jacket and pullover sweater and felt checkered hat came in. "Well, is that a way to sell your paper! By using your girlfriend to be on the front cover."

"Irwin, you old son of a gun." He held out his bandaged hand but Irwin waved it away.

He rested again on the pillow and said to B.J., "Wanna get married, baby?"

"Only if I can cater it."

"Well, I'll leave you two lovebirds to pitch and woo."

"Leave but give us a break."

"I finally took that vacation I had planned. I got a fishing rod and some high boots and I need to pick up some hunting gear and I'll be okay. Better marry her before someone else does. She's a beauty, I always thought that. Only you could do without the blond hair."

Somewhere Wilton Stronger was being laid to rest and so was B.J.'s past.

"Will you marry me, B.J.?"

"Yes," she said. "Is this the happily-ever-after part, Joe?"

"Only if I hear that laugh."

Irwin laughed, enjoying this.

"The mushy part," he said. "This is where I chill

217

out. Listen, I left my wife and kids to go fishing and hunting and riding. And I have to come back with a tan."

"A tan in September?"

"No, actually, I'm covering this story for the *Post*. SLEEPING BEAUTY WAKES UP."

"Incredible. What about the answering machine?" Joe said to her.

"Well, from now on I'll say 'B.J. Stronger.' "

"You'll say 'B.J. Peterson,' is what you'll say," Irwin said.

"You know, baby, I always hated those things," Joe said, and smiling and holding her hand, he fell asleep.